MR
PERFECT

by
Joanna Davies

HONNO MODERN FICTION

First published in the English language by Honno Press in 2013
'Ailsa Craig', Heol y Cawl, Dinas Powys, South Glamorgan, Wales, CF64
4AH

1 2 3 4 5 6 7 8 9 10

A catalogue record for this book is available from the British Library.

Published with the financial support of the Welsh Books Council.

ISBN 9781906784676
Cover design: Sam Novak
Text design: Elaine Sharples
Printed in Wales by Gomer Press

For Steven

Acknowledgements

Thanks to: my editor, Caroline Oakley, and the team at Honno and to my readers.

Prologue

Mari

Do you choose your fate, or does fate choose for you? Is the perfect man out there waiting for you to hook him like a skilled fisherman, or are you relying on finding a pitiful creature that's reasonably suitable within your own square mile? Perhaps that magical man with George Clooney's velvet eyes, Johnny Depp's cheekbones, Brad Pitt's smile and body (yes, the body he has in *Fight Club*, where he wears that awful dressing gown) and Christian Slater's sexy arrogance in *Heathers*, is living in Japan or Tahiti. If that's the case you'll never meet him even though he exists somewhere out there.

Travelling on the bus, the car or walking down the street, the single amongst you dream that you might be jogging or driving past Mr Perfect that very second and that any minute now there'll be a 'meet cute' situation, exactly like there is in Hollywood. You could be stuck in a lift together, or he could come to your rescue when someone steals your handbag in town. Or you might meet at a party, and he might accidentally spill red wine over your best party frock and have to make it up to you. What if you knocked him off his bike whilst driving? You might both fall in love across the courtroom while he's suing you for dangerous driving... More likely you'll meet in a random bar at the end of an evening, when you're like that desperate woman at the Topshop sale, determined to get your hands on anything, anything but go home empty handed – other than with chips from the local take-away. Do you settle for Mr Will Just About Do, or is fate so bloody brilliant that you will find the man of your dreams on your doorstep? And what about the one that escaped your clutches? Was he really a dud or, and here's a frightening possibility, was he a stud?

Now that I'm 33 years old, almost reaching my prime (according to Miss Jean Brodie), it's time for me to stop dreaming about that perfect man, the handsome knight and his big white steed – the laughable Barbara Cartland, Jane Austen, Bridget Jones cliché, which, in my opinion, still fills even the most fervent feminist's imagination. But this mythical creature is like the elusive snow leopard, almost extinct. As I sit at my untidy office desk, pretending to write a document to sell a new TV leisure series, *House and Garden*, I think about why I find it hard to stay in a relationship for more than two years, (I'm too impatient to wait for the seven year itch). I come to the conclusion that perhaps I'm to blame more than them.

Me with my foolish, unreal, romantic desires which took root in my brain and heart years ago, thanks to watching too many romantic films in my teens (thank you *Gone With The Wind*, *The Princess Bride* and *Dirty Dancing*). I have to remember that real men don't behave like Laurence Olivier as the dashing Lord Nelson in *That Hamilton Woman*. It's the writer's fantasy that makes him say those magical words as he is about to kiss her on New Year's Eve 1799. "My love, now I have kissed you through two centuries." His real-life wife, the immortal Vivien Leigh, then at the height of her beauty, was playing Lady Hamilton, which must have made it easier to be truly convincing. Gary Oldman's honeyed words as sexy Dracula to the nubile Winona Ryder: "I have crossed oceans of time to be with you," are also pure fantasy. And a Patrick Swayze type won't be strutting up to me in black leathers muttering the infamous words, "No-one puts baby in the corner…" It's time for me, Mari Wyn Roberts, to grow up and stop looking for Mr Perfect. Because he might, just might, have been hiding under my nose the whole time despite 15 years of relentless searching. Wouldn't that be a tragedy and a comedy, both?

Owen

I don't know what's wrong with me. Why did I finish with Lucy? She was perfect for me... OK, she was a psycho and in bed she was like a turkey waiting to be stuffed – not a lot of "go" in her. But that's the best I could get, as Lucy herself told me when I finished with her. I tried my best to get her to finish with me, but nothing doing. I tried to ignore the endless texts, the incessant pokes on Facebook, the relentless pleading to go on holiday to Venice... I tried everything to make her understand that we had no future. That we didn't really suit each other... But she was like a fly in jam – stuck on me, until in the end I had to get the police involved... What I want is a woman with Kelly Brook's body, Dawn French's humour and Carol Vorderman's brains. Is that too much to ask?

I'm starting to get desperate. I've thought about putting my details down on Cwtsh.com, the Welsh dating site, but then *everybody* would know I was desperate and more than likely, I'd probably have had a liaison with them before, Wales is that kind of place so small everyone knows everyone, or at least somebody who knows someone. I'm 33 years old, 7 out of 10 in looks, 8, with a bit of work, no kids, with a nice flat in Cardiff Bay, what else do they need? I'm sensitive (sometimes), play guitar, with an OK job. Why doesn't anyone want me? What's wrong with me? Where is she?

I always thought I'd have found somebody by now. Turning 30 plus and fumbling around in noisy clubs for your soulmate really scares me. There's nothing worse than desperate middle-aged men slobbering over teenage girls. I might as well grow a comb-over, wear Old Spice and a medallion. I *don't* want to be one of those saddos that Huw and I used to laugh at when we were younger. I have to be more positive. It isn't too late and as Mum says, every failed relationship should help me understand what I really want in a life partner, or a girlfriend that lasts more than two months. I don't want a clingy girl, she has to be fit, she has to be clever (not cleverer than me, but with a good degree). I feel that I'm in *Weird Science* trying to create the perfect girl; a pity that's not possible, it would be much easier

Did I do the right thing leaving Lucy? After all, she was a "safe pair of glands" as Huw put it. But I have to resist looking back at that awful relationship with rose tinted spectacles. Things can only get better and if I don't look too hard, then she's bound to appear, under my nose, just like in the movies – well, a man can dream…

Chapter 1

Mari

Mr Cool, 1992

A beautiful 18-year-old girl walked confidently down the school corridor. She was stunning; tall and elegant, her long blonde hair flowing down her back. Her brown, shapely legs emerged from tiny shorts and her aquamarine eyes made people stop for a second look. She opened her locker to collect her school books and jumped as she felt a hand squeeze her breast cheekily. "Dylan!" she squeaked with laughter as he embraced her passionately whilst the other kids stared at them open mouthed.

Mari switched off the TV impatiently. *Beverly Hills 90210* was really immature and the main characters, who were meant to be in their teens, looked older than her mum and dad! She had to stop watching this crap so she'd have enough time to get ready. She'd been looking forward to this party for ages. And for one reason: James Rees. Or J.R. as everyone called him. J.R. filled her mind day and night. At 16, J.R. was the "catch" of the school. And like a slippery eel, he'd managed to avoid any long term relationships with his numerous admirers, and as a result, his surprising availability had inspired Mari to give him the main role in her romantic fantasies. James would definitely be at the party as it was his big sister's 18th at the local rugby club. Mari, along with her fellow Fifth Form students, had been invited to what would be her first 18th birthday party. She hoped she'd get the chance to dance with James tonight. Only one dance, just one, in his strong arms. Mari loved his green eyes, his silky dark hair, his muscly and solid body… J.R. was the hero of the rugby team, the brightest student in his year. Everyone loved J.R. If he were a character in a film his strapline would be "The boys wanted to be J.R. and the girls wanted J.R." There's one of these magical creatures in every school; the mythical unicorn amongst the donkeys, the one that looks cool whatever, the one that stands out amidst the crowd of acne, sweat and mullets; the perfect boy. But Mari knew she wasn't perfect.

Since her first day in secondary school, Mari had known she was different to the other girls. A swot, a nerd and an eccentric, just like Winona Ryder's oddball character, Veronica, in Mari's favourite film, *Heathers*, in which Winona and a dashing Christian Slater murdered several of their obnoxious school mates. She was sensitive and could offer more to a boy like James than the shallow bimbos at school. So obsessed was she with Winona's character in this dark movie that, like her heroine, Mari had bought a monocle to make herself look more interesting. And the monocle would come out when she sang in the school choir, to the disgust of their tuneless and egocentric music teacher and the jeers of her mainstream classmates. Yes, Leia's birthday party would be the perfect opportunity to show J.R. that his ideal woman had been waiting for him like a bug in a chrysalis, about to be transformed into a stunningly sexy butterfly. She looked at the clock, five already. Sara would be picking her up in two hours!

Sara's mum was a very generous chauffeur to them both. Mari's mum didn't care for her daughter's predilection for gigs and parties and was reluctant to offer her a lift – apart from the numerous weekly trips to harp, piano, singing and drama teachers. "You need to focus on your schoolwork at your age, madam, not cavorting with boys!" her mother kept telling her. Thank God, Sara's mum was cool and appreciated the fact that Mari's mum had had instruction on parental guidance from Atilla the Hun.

When Mari turned 16 – a dangerous sexual milestone – her mother had asked her into her bedroom for a chat. "I've got something to show you," her mum said, taking out an old baby's shawl from the secret drawer under her bed. Wrapped securely in the shawl were dozens of sharp and pointy metal staples. Mari looked at them aghast. She'd hoped her mum was going to give her the antique gold bracelet she had squirreled away in her jewellery box, not a collection of rusty old staples.

"These, my girl, are what the doctor used to hold my abdomen shut when you were born." Between 1968 and 1972, her mum had given birth to two kids relatively smoothly but when it came time for Mari to fight her way through the birth canal in 1976, several life-threatening complications had led to her fatigued mother opting for a bloody and painful emergency Caesarean.

"If you want to have relations with a boy, then remember these staples and what might happen if you're tempted, Mari. Men only want one thing and they'll say anything to get it. Nobody gives cheese to a mouse after catching it, remember." Her mother's small blue eyes looked into Mari's as she held the staples under Mari's nose.

Having "relations" with a boy? Chance would be a fine thing, Mari thought to herself bitterly. She hadn't even had her first kiss yet, let alone anything else! Who did her mother think Mari was? Those numerous nerdy extra-curricular activities were the kiss of death; the boys in school either treated her like one of the boys, or like a nerd or a freak. Or, worse still, completely ignored her, whilst making out with the more conventional girls in the cloakrooms at lunchtime. The staples sat in her mum's drawer like artefacts from the Black Museum, but their image was burnt into Mari's memory and she'd decided that she never, *never*, wanted to have a baby. The thought of something alive growing inside you was like something out of Ridley Scott's *Alien*.

It was weird that her mum had so many hang-ups about sex and babies, bearing in mind that she'd had three kids, Mari mused. When naked ladies appeared on the TV, there would be a deathly silence in the sitting room, with even the tumbleweed beating a swift exit behind the sofa. Mari's dad (a quiet and laid back man) would be quite happily watching Benny Hill's perky maidens chasing the smut master around the park on the small screen, but her mum would soon start tutting under her breath saying, "Jim! *Songs of Praise* is on now, turn it over!" And when they'd started watching *The Graduate* recently, her mum nearly had a fit when the naked showgirl appeared, waving the colourful tassels on her nipples with gay abandon. "Jim! Go upstairs, you need to bleed the radiator!" she commanded, changing the channel directly.

Anyhoo, Mari had gained her mum's permission to attend tonight's party after a long discussion that resembled a UN meeting. Sara's mum had promised she'd pick up the girls at 11pm sharp and that Mari would be home safely by 11.30pm. There wouldn't be any alcohol served to under-18s as J.R.'s dad would be serving behind the bar. But Mari's mum was unaware that Sara would be hiding a stash of Thunderbird wine in her bag. She and Mari had sneaked to the corner shop to buy it ready for this special occasion. "We'll have a few swigs of the wine before going in", Sara had whispered to Mari in drama that afternoon. "And we'll ask for lemonade from the bar so we can mix it in the toilets. Nobody will be any the wiser!"

Mari looked at her reflection proudly. The new dress she'd bought from Winky's second hand clothes shop in Swansea had been worth every penny. It was lacy, short and very flattering. With it she wore bright red Doc Marten boots and black tights and strings of pearls as accessories like her idol, Madonna. Her make-up was subtle for now, in case her mum had a fit, but she could add more eyeliner and lippy in the car. Madonna was crooning Mari's favourite song, "Crazy for You", on the stereo as she got ready. Mari hoped it would be the accompaniment to her dance with J.R. It was almost 7pm and she could hear Sara's mum's horn tooting outside, the fanfare to a night to remember.

"Remember to be home by half past eleven!" her mum shouted at her from the sitting room as she ran out of the house like a whirlwind.

"Yes, Mum, you've told me loads of times!"

"And no drinking! I'll be waiting up to check that you're sober!"

"Okay, Mum! Ta-ra!"

Mari forgot everything about her mother and her warning as she jumped into Sara's mother's luxurious car. Sara sat by her side, full of excitement. Mari looked at Sara without a modicum of jealousy. Sara was one of those girls that all the boys fancied; small and busty, with a Catherine Zeta Jones-like sex appeal. Sara's boyfriend, David Jones, a 6th former, was recovering from a rugby injury so he wouldn't be at the party, thank God. Sara would be at her side all night, well, at least until Mari got her hooks into J.R.

"Hey, that frock looks cool on you", Sara said looking at Mari with the thoroughness of a forensic scientist.

"Not as nice as yours!" Mari said, looking enviously at Sara's new red mini dress.

"I don't know why you girls waste your money on these old 60s' rags," Sara's mother laughed. "I've got plenty of gear you could have for free in the attic!"

"They stink of mothballs, Mum," Sara said.

"Well, that's better than stinking of sweat like those rags you girls have got on tonight!" Mrs Lewis replied.

Sara gave Mari a cheeky poke in her ribs and discreetly showed her the contents of her handbag, and inside, like the Holy Grail, the Thunderbird bottle glinted. Mari opened her handbag just as discreetly and revealed the pack of Malboro Reds she'd hidden there.

"You girls are wound up tonight!" Mrs Lewis said as

the girls giggled mischievously. "Remember to behave yourselves and be ready for me to pick you up at 11pm on the dot. I don't want to anger your mum, Mari!"

"OK, Mum," Sara said. "We'll be like nerdy Cinderellas leaving before midnight. Everybody else will be staying until the party finishes."

"Don't whinge," her mum replied with a smile. "You're 16. 11pm is more than fair. If I hear any more complaints, I'll be there at ten!"

"Ok mum! 11 o'clock will be fine!"

"Thanks for the lift, Mrs Lewis."

"No problem, Mari. When I'm old and frail, I'm hoping madam here will give me a lift or two!"

"No, Mum, the nurses in the old folks home will be able to do that for you, I'm sure!" Sara chortled and Mrs Lewis joined in the joke.

Mari was envious of the easy-going relationship between Sara and her mum. Mrs Lewis was cool, had gone to university in the Swinging Sixties and gave more than enough freedom to her daughter.

"Right, here we are!" Mrs Lewis announced as they drove into the Rugby Club car park. There were lots of people arriving.

"See you later, Mum!" Sara trilled, as she and Mari scrambled out of the car.

"No thank yous?".

"Thanks, Mrs Lewis!"

"Cheers, Ma!"

Sara put a comradely arm through Mari's as they approached the club. The air even smelt different tonight – OK Mari could smell chips and cheap aftershave, but there was something intangible too – she wasn't sure what it was but she knew it was thrilling! A gaggle of teenagers was walking in ahead of them and Sara was already vetting the girls' outfits:

"Look at the state on that Samantha Jones over there," Sara stage-whispered as she rolled her eyes towards a rather rotund classmate. She'd obviously taken Madonna as her inspiration for the evening – but the *Desperately Seeking Susan* years: she was adorned in a lacy black mini-dress, over-sized leather jacket and an abundance of bracelets and chains, including a large gaudy pink crucifix around her neck. Mari was pleased that she'd gone for a "low key look" – she wanted to be classy as she presumed J.R. wouldn't go for tacky looking girls; well, as far as she knew, he hadn't been out with any of them in the past.

As they walked towards the Club, Mari looked around, hoping to see J.R. amongst the newcomers. But she couldn't see him anywhere. "Where's J.R?"

"He must have arrived already," Sara said calmly. "After all, it is his sister's party. Now, Mari, try and be cool for God's sake. There's nothing worse than a desperate woman you know! They can smell it!"

"I won't talk to him until 8.30," Mari said. Though she was yearning to go and speak to J.R. as soon as possible.

"Yes, give it an hour at least. You'll have had a chance to pluck up some Dutch courage by then," Sara said, dragging her to the bar. The Rugby Club was quite full already. There were numerous 18 banners and balloons adorning the rather scruffy dance hall. The DJ was playing cheesy records and the birthday girl was greeting her guests happily.

"Should we go and say happy birthday to her?" Mari asked Sara.

"Pfft! I doubt she gives a shit one way or another… It's not as if we had a special invitation or anything…"

"Well, it seems a bit rude just to eat her food and not say anything…"

"God, Mari, you worry about everything. We'll say hello later when she isn't surrounded. Let's get something to drink, I'm gasping!"

As they waited in the queue for the bar, Mari felt the hairs on the back of her neck quivering. *He* must be nearby. She turned her head and from the corner of her eye saw J.R. helping his dad carry boxes of ale behind the bar. It was obvious the party wasn't going to be an alcohol free zone, Mari thought with relief. After all, it was an 18th birthday party.

J.R. looked stunning. He wore a T-shirt that showed

off his muscles and tight 501 jeans on his long legs. His hair was still wet from the shower, Mari thought as she stared intently at him. It was always weird to see him outside the school scenario and not in uniform, less real somehow. She watched him walk towards his sister. If there was a soundtrack to this scene in a film, it would definitely be "Take My Breath Away" by Berlin; cheesy but a classic...

"Stop staring at him, will you!" Sara sighed. "Don't be so obvious!" Mari reluctantly turned her attention back to her friend.

"Right, girls," J.R's dad beamed at them from behind the bar, "what's your poison? Lemonade, orange juice or Coke?"

"We were hoping for a small glass of wine please, Mr Rees." Sara winked at him. She was shameless, flirting with an old man like Mr Rees, he must be forty at least! Mari thought to herself.

"Now then Sara, you know very well you can't have wine. If you're good girls, then I might sneak you a shandy later!"

"Two lemonades then, please, Mr Rees", Sara said feigning disappointment. As they carried their glasses towards the toilets, Sara said, "Well, the apple doesn't fall far from the tree! Mr Rees is hot!"

"Sara, he's way too old for you. And he's married!"

"So?" Sara said, nonchalantly. "David is boring me

with his rugby obsession. I've always fancied an affair with a more experienced man like Mr Rees!"

"Sara!" Mari said, her eyes gleaming with shock and envy. "Wouldn't you be terrified?" Mari wished she was as daring as Sara, she was too scared to approach a schoolboy like J.R. let alone proposition an older man!

"They all have the same equipment, Mari fach!" Sara chuckled as they squeezed their way into a toilet cubicle together. Sara pulled the Thunderbird bottle out of her bag and started pouring the sickly sweet wine into their lemonade glasses. That was the main difference between Sara and Mari. Sara was already sexually experienced. She'd lost her virginity when she was 15 years old, to David her current lover, and she'd had a few flings whilst on holiday abroad. According to Sara, sex was pleasant enough, once you got used to the initial discomfort and got over the shock that the penis behaved like a creature independent of its master. Half past eight had come and gone and Sara and Mari sat near the buffet table watching their fellow pupils devouring the mini sausages and pizzas and the sticky vol-au-vents. Mari was bursting to speak to James but his friends were still surrounding him. *"Sara!"* she *whispered to her friend. "It's nine o'clock!"*

"Yeah, and…?" Sara said casually, busy making eyes at one of the 6th form boys who was blushing in response.

"I want to speak to James! But he's never on his own!"

"Listen. Wait for a bit until everyone goes to dance and then we can dance by his side and I'll pull him to dance with you".

"What help will that be?" Mari asked unwillingly. "He'll start dancing with you then!"

"No, no. Duh!" Sara said impatiently. "I, by then, Mrs Stupid, will be dancing with Rhys from the 6th form!"

"But what about David?"

"It's perfectly fine for me to dance with other boys, Mari," Sara said patronisingly. "David and I aren't married you know and Rhys is cute!"

"OK," Mari said more hopeful now, because Sara always got her way with men.

"Now, you need to relax before we go up to him. Time for another little Thunderbird I think!" Sara discreetly poured them both a generous slug of wine under the table and lit up a Marlboro Red, puffing it as blasé as Marlene Dietrich in her heyday.

"Sara, don't!" Mari whispered.

"What's the problem?" Sara laughed at her, blowing smoke rings up at the ceiling. "It's only JR's dad and he's smoking as well! We're 16 you know, old enough to do a lot of things! Not just fags." She smirked as she necked her wine.

"Right, go and ask the DJ to put on a really good song."

"Like what?"

"Something to get them dancing, of course, so we can kick off our plan to entice J.R.!"

Mari pushed her way impatiently through the crowd. Bloody hell, most of them were pissed already! It was stiflingly hot on the dance floor and most of the kids were glugging their drinks with abandon, resulting in copious spillages. Mari dodged one particularly drunk sixth former who almost spilt a whole pint over her!

Finally she reached the DJ and politely asked, "Can you play 'Crazy for You' by Madonna please?"

"Eh? I can't hear you love," the DJ replied. He had a big black 'tache like a 70s' porn star.

"'Crazy for You' by Madonna, please?"

"Sorry, haven't got that, lovely. What about a bit of Abba?"

Damn it! Her fantasies of dancing to "Crazy for You" with James were ruined! She walked back sulkily to Sara. Who wanted to dance to Abba? But to her great surprise, when the familiar intro to "Dancing Queen" started playing, everyone got up to dance.

"Good choice, Mari," Sara said as she dragged her towards James.

As she approached him, Mari started to shake. Who did she think she was, trying to pull this gorgeous specimen? He looked even more unbearably handsome close up. Shit, one more second and she'd be in his eyeline. She couldn't do it! "I don't want to, Sara!" Mari said tugging at her friend's sleeve. But Sara couldn't hear her over the loud music. Before she could beat a retreat, James was being pulled towards her by Sara and he was coming along quite obediently. Sara winked at Mari and placed James in front of her like a dog with a stick. And, true to her word, immediately disappeared in the direction of Rhys from the Sixth form.

James smiled at Mari as he danced at her side. Mari smiled back awkwardly. Shit! She was a crap dancer but here she was, living her dream at last. James was obviously happy to hold on to her as they danced and slowly yet surely Mari began to feel more confident, thanks to the magic powers of the Thunderbird, and grabbed hold of him too. Oh my God, she could feel the muscles of his arms, so strong, so masculine… His aftershave smelt delicious – Calvin Klein's ck one if she wasn't mistaken. No cheap Lynx muck for JR! Everyone around them faded into the background, as if they were dancing in slow motion. She could only see J.R and his gorgeous face, his mesmerising eyes pulling her in deeper and deeper…

"You look really pretty tonight, Mari."

"Thanks, and you," Mari answered, unable to believe she'd said such a thing. That was even worse than Baby's faux pas when she met Patrick Swayze for the first time in *Dirty Dancing* when she was roped in to lugging a massive watermelon to a secret party where all the cool

21

dancer kids hung out. But thankfully she didn't think he'd heard her as he smiled and gulped some of his beer. As the song came to an end and Mari looked at James. He'd probably go back to his friends now. But no, he stayed at her side and tenderly held her face and started to snog her! Oh my God! He was kissing her! Her first kiss and with James Rees! Was this a dream? She didn't know what to do! How to breathe, or when to breathe? Was that a tongue? She felt the stubble on his chin pushing her chin. Her legs were like jelly and she felt the earth spinning beneath her feet. Shit! She should have eaten a mint or something before kissing him. Did her breath taste disgusting? Of fags and Thunderbird? James's breath smelt a bit of lager but that didn't matter to her. Should she stick her tongue in his mouth too? Argh! She was out of her depth! She'd just have to mimic him and hope for the best. She hadn't asked Sara for any kissing tips as she hadn't properly envisaged getting this near JR tonight, let alone being kissed by him!

"Fancy some fresh air?" James whispered in her ear.

"OK!" Mari said, hardly believing her luck as he pulled her unceremoniously out of the Club towards the car park. James pulled out a pack of cigarettes from his jacket and offered her one. It was a pity that he didn't light it for her like Paul Henreid did in *Now Voyager*, Mari thought to herself. That was so romantic – lighting two cigarettes at once, in one easy move and then giving Bette

Davis one of them – so smooth! But she couldn't have everything. She had James for tonight and that was more than enough. They smoked their cigarettes slowly and James pulled her towards him for another kiss. Her breasts were crushed up against his muscled chest as they French kissed and Mari felt a combination of fear and lust flood her body.

"I've fancied you for a while, Mari," James whispered in her ear.

"Have…have you?" Mari said thinking that this was a dream and at any minute her alarm clock would ring and she'd wake up.

"And, I've noticed you looking at me too," James said, teasingly, as he pulled her into a dark corner in the car park.

"Perhaps I have…" Mari played coy, trying to remember Sara's tips on how to flirt with boys.

"I've always thought you were different… different to the other girls," he said, looking into her eyes. If she'd given him a script to read, she couldn't have improved on his words. They kissed more passionately this time. But then J.R. grabbed her hand and placed it on his crotch. Oh my God, he had a full on stiffy! Ew! She really didn't know what she was supposed to do. She patted it feebly and then returned her hand to the safety of his chest and kissed him, hoping he wouldn't flag up the *protuberance* in his pants again. Suddenly, he pulled away and Mari saw James groping in his pocket for something.

Mari watched in growing horror as she saw the Durex packet glinting at her. Oh my God! She hadn't expected this! In her imagination, she'd seen James and her walking hand in hand on the beach the Sunday after the party, James teaching her to play tennis, embracing her after winning a rugby match… And then in a few months and in a luxurious bedroom, with her legs shaved, she'd lose her virginity to him. Not this, not a quickie in a dirty car park… How the hell could she get herself out of this unfortunate situation without offending him? There was only one way out and as J.R. turned away to put the condom on his penis, Mari bent double.

"I feel ill!" she said sighing. And carefully she fell to the floor. She closed her eyes tightly, hoping he'd go away and fetch help, preferably Sara. She sensed James standing above her staring at her. He shook her shoulder roughly and yelled, "Mari!" in her ear but she kept her eyes tightly closed. "Mari!" he shouted louder this time, but no dice. After a few seconds of silence, she heard him grunt under his breath, "Fuckin' waste of time!" Then she heard the snap of the condom as he pulled it unceremoniously off his penis followed by the sound of the zip of his jeans being pulled up. She opened her eyes as she heard him walking away from her and back into the rugby club, tears flowing down her cheeks. She got to her feet and looked at her watch. Half past ten. Another half an hour and she'd be safely home.

Owen

Miss Pin-up, 1992

Owen's hands were shaking nervously as he tried to shave the tiny awkward hairs from his neck. "Fuck!" he exclaimed in pain as the sharp razor cut a small bloody wound. Typical! He was preparing to go out with the girl of every Fernhill Comprehensive School boys' dreams, the girl of *his* dreams, and he had to cut a bit of his face off whilst shaving! *Right, don't sweat, a smidge of Brut on it and the fucker would stop bleeding. Oof!* Adding the Brut wasn't a good idea as the blood and chemicals mixed in a stinging cocktail. Now, for his hair. Owen had spent all his pocket money on a stylish new haircut from Toni and Guy in town, but it was worth every penny, as the spikes on his head resembled in his eyes, a clump of majestic coral under the sea… A bit of gel, not too much, some more Lynx under his armpits and in his underpants and he'd be ready. Oof! That was another mistake – he'd forgotten that he'd given a polite trim to his pubes yesterday, just in case, through some miracle, they might make an appearance tonight. He didn't want Michelle to think he was keeping one of Chewbacca's descendants in his Calvin's. He was really chuffed with his new black jeans, Levi 501s of course and his new smart grey shirt from Topman. He stared at himself in the mirror. The blood was drying on his chin and he hoped Michelle wouldn't notice it. Yes, he was ready. But was he good enough for Michelle? Would she think he was pathetic?

Michelle Richards. He had to face facts; she should be out of his league completely. With her beautiful golden hair, her sexy aquamarine eyes and her shapely body (the result of gymnastic feats in numerous school tournaments) she was everyone's pin-up; even the Headmaster would blush a bright beetroot red when he came across Michelle. Huw, Owen's best mate, had bet him that he wouldn't have the guts to ask Michelle out. And he didn't know why he did such a thing, perhaps, because everyone in the 6th form common room had overhead Huw's challenge and was waiting to see if he'd pick up the gauntlet. His heart started to race again as he relived that crucial moment when he'd walked up to her to ask her out on a date. She was sat on the sofa with her friends, licking a pink Chupa Chups lollipop. The whole incident remained crystal clear and played out in slow motion in his memory… Was it misguided kindness or pity that made her accept? Well, that was Huw and the rest of the envious 6th form boys' theory, or was it because she knew that he was her perfect man?

He rooted around in his sock drawer to find the packet

of three. He'd deliberated for a while before choosing a suitable brand of condom for this date. He'd decided to go with the "gold deluxe" – because as Huw said, "You can't skimp where Michelle is in the frame." He'd bought two packets and had used one up in a trial run to ensure that he would be able to put the latex sock on his penis in a deft manner, so that Michelle wouldn't discover his complete lack of experience in the sexual arena. He placed the packet of condoms carefully in his coat pocket. He took one more look at his reflection and said in a Robert De Niro-like voice, "Right then boys, I'm going in!" Tonight he was representing all the 6th form boys, all the boys in Wales, perhaps all the boys in the world, in his attempt to seduce the perfect woman…

"Oh my God, it's George Michael!" Owen's younger sister, Megan, chortled as she surveyed him in the kitchen.

"Piss off!" Owen turned to his mum and pleaded, "Mum, can I have the car keys please? You said I could take it out after passing my test…"

Owen's mum was busy washing up and turned to look at her son, "Don't swear at your sister, Owen. Well, you do look quite respectable tonight. Who's the lucky young lady?"

"Michelle Richards," Megan said with a smug grin.

Oh for fuck's sake! Couldn't she keep her big trap shut?

"Michelle Richards, isn't she that pretty blonde you

27

were mooning over last year?" Owen's dad was reading the newspaper but obviously was listening intently to the conversation.

"Yes, Dad and I need the car to take her out tonight…"

"Owen, you scraped both sides of the Metro the last time you took it out." His mum looked at him dubiously.

"Oh, leave the boy be Bethan, he needs some wheels to impress his date," Owen's dad tossed the keys at him.

"Thanks, Dad."

"Well, just be careful with the car and no monkey business in the back seat!" his mum admonished.

"Ugh!" Megan said.

"Mum!" Owen rolled his eyes at his family as they started to chortle at his mum's joke. Monkey business indeed! He should be so lucky!

Owen beeped his car horn playfully as he waited outside Michelle's house. Bloody hell, he better not prang the car tonight, he'd had to beg his mum and dad to be allowed to take it out on his own for the first time. His mum still remembered too well that time when he scraped the sides of her Austin Metro when he tried to reverse it out of their drive a few months ago. She'd even refused to come driving with him after that!

Michelle's house was, as he expected, a luxurious suburban palace in Roath, Cardiff, a stone's throw from the lake. A month had gone by since he'd passed his driving test and he was still really nervous behind the wheel. He'd have to fake it with Michelle that he was an experienced driver as he'd heard from Huw that she had been out with some college boys in her time who probably had really slick cars that they could drive like Nigel Mansel! He'd chosen "cool" music to play on his tape player in the car – Dépèche Mode and had got rid of Madonna and Phil Collins from his driving-music collection. He'd planned on taking her to a posh Indian restaurant in town and, of course, being the perfect gentleman he would pay for everything.

Close-up Michelle's house was even more impressive. A gargantuan door, painted a threatening pillar box red with a snarling lion door-knocker, massive bay windows – obviously Victorian (his mum would be very impressed to learn his new girlfriend lived in one of these posh houses). His own house was nice but just a normal semi, not a towering townhouse like this one. He was out of his league in every way! The fear returned to his heart as the front door of her house opened and Michelle stepped out. The halo of dim streetlight briefly transformed her into an angel as she ran towards his car. But then he clocked her white leather jacket and short denim mini skirt, this girl was no angel! She wore cowboy boots which displayed her shapely brown legs perfectly. Owen could feel his nether regions stirring in his underpants. *For God's sake, get a grip*! he told his disobedient organ.

Michelle opened the door and jumped in.

"Hiya!" she breathed, kissing him on the cheek.

"Hiya."

"Where are you taking me, then?" Michelle asked, pulling a half bottle of wine out of her handbag and drinking lustily.

Owen was surprised to see her toting the wine. He'd thought she was a sophisticated girl, not someone who got pissed on Thunderbird. Perhaps she might be nervous too and wanted a bit of Dutch courage? Yes, that was the reason for the booze in the bag, wasn't it? Or did she want to get pissed so she could face kissing him later?

"Well, I was thinking of a nice dinner at the Golden Palace, in town".

"Indian? With all those empty calories? No thanks! Just drive into the park here so we can chat for a bit," Michelle commanded.

Owen obeyed, although his heart was sinking. She obviously didn't want to be seen in public with him. He started to fear that this date might have been a "wind-up" all along. A sinister plot that she and her bitchy mates had dreamed up to take the piss out of him.

"Park here!" Michelle said as they pulled into the park near the lake.

"Don't you want to go out somewhere…the cinema perhaps?" Owen asked as he turned off the car engine.

"We don't need to go anywhere do we? We've got

everything we need here..." Michelle offered a cigarette to Owen. Owen took it, his heart beating like a drum.

He didn't know what she wanted from him. He looked at her drinking her Thunderbird wine and lighting her ciggy with the flick of an expert.

"What do you mean, Michelle?"

"Well, comfortable seats, Thunderbird, fags... Have you got condoms?"

Did she just ask him for condoms? He swallowed the spittle that had been collecting in his mouth and said weakly, "Erm... yes... But don't you want to talk a bit first?"

"Talk? Talk about what?" Michelle asked as she put her dainty little feet up on the dashboard. God, even her feet turned him on!

Owen felt like a mongoose ensnared by a snake but tried to buy some time, "Well, your interests... I don't really know you very well." He took a deep drag on his cigarette to calm his nerves and felt the hot sour smoke in his chest. Ugh! He hated cigarettes.

Michelle laughed as she blew a perfect smoke-ring around her head. "What do you mean? We've been in school together for ages! Listen, take a swig of this and you won't be so shy!" Michelle passed him the Thunderbird bottle and Owen took one small sip before returning it to her. "Take more than that!"

"No, I better not. I've only just passed my test."

Michelle looked at him for a few seconds before taking her coat off. Owen noticed she was wearing a very low cut top, which showed her perfect breasts most effectively. And then, completely unexpectedly she took off her jumper and sat there just in her lacy pink bra and skirt. Oh my God! She was obviously a sex maniac! What about foreplay? He thought girls wanted chat and flirtation first, then, if you were lucky, around the third date, according to Huw, who'd had it on good authority from his elder brother Dan, a blow job perhaps. Not the "full Monty" on the first date, in a park! He hadn't really planned on having to use those condoms tonight! What if he wasn't hard enough…or even worse, what if he came too quickly? Shit! Why hadn't he taken Huw's advice and had a practice run with someone else? You didn't drive a Rolls Royce before practising in a Skoda first!

Michelle was staring at him. He had to take the lead, show he was up for it before she got fed up. He pulled off his seatbelt and leaned towards her and started kissing her, slowly. Then he could feel her tongue in his mouth and her hand on his crotch! His penis was on fire, yearning to be freed from its imprisonment inside his pants. His head was spinning. This was heaven and hell at the same time! How could he keep control of himself? It was as if Michelle had been reading his mind and she started to undo his jeans. Owen looked at her in surprise as she kept kissing his neck whilst undoing his jeans nimbly. She was obviously a pro. Her dexterity had to be the result of much practice.

"Jump in the back with me!" Michelle ordered as she sprung into the back seat like a horny gazelle.

Owen struggled to join her with his jeans hanging awkwardly around his thighs. His penis now had forgotten any sense of decorum and was standing upright in his pants like a pole. Shit! He'd forgotten about the gold deluxe in his coat pocket. His coat was on the floor by the driver's seat. Before he had a chance to fetch it, Michelle's arms were around him like a vice as she snogged his face off. She ripped his shirt open – he couldn't believe she was such an animal. Huw and the boys would never believe it!

"That's it, don't be shy," Michelle murmured as she grabbed his penis authoritatively. He could feel it bucking like a frightened rabbit. Then her head moved down to his crotch and as her mouth closed in and she began sucking eagerly, Owen realised the true purpose of the lollipops that Michelle was constantly licking at school. After an initial battle to avoid coming immediately in her mouth, something he feared with his whole being, a new feeling rose up in him. *Shit, he wasn't going to…was he?* He could feel the nausea building up in his stomach – was it a combination of shock, Thunderbird or the ciggy he'd smoked that had led to this? He tried in vain to push Michelle's head away but she mistook this for enthusiasm on his part and sucked harder.

"*Oh fuck!* Bleurgh!"

Everything froze in a tableau for a few seconds as Michelle spat him out in shock and disbelief. Her perfect mane of golden hair was a fright wig of regurgitated carrots and tomatoes.

"Oh my God! What the fuck's wrong with you, you pig? There's sick all over me! Shit!"

Owen couldn't believe it. Out of all the scenarios that had played in his head about the crucial moment when he'd lose his virginity to Michelle, he'd never imagined that he'd vomit over her! Was there any way to rescue the situation? He fumbled in his jeans awkwardly as Michelle hastily got dressed.

"I'm really sorry. I must have eaten something that didn't agree with me... An egg sarnie or something. Look, I've got a hanky." He offered her an old bedraggled handkerchief with a trembling hand. Michelle grabbed the tissue from him and tried unsuccessfully to wipe her hair clean.

"You're mental, you know that? The girls all said I was mental to go off with a weirdo like you! Knobhead!" She grabbed her coat, her bag and the bottle of Thunderbird and got out of the car in a hell of a temper.

"Michelle!" Owen shouted after her. But he knew he wouldn't get another chance. Like a fairy tale character, she'd returned to her ivory tower and left him there with vomit stained pants and a broken heart. This would mean the end of his sex life until he left school and probably Wales! Roxette's cheesy ballad "It Must Have Been Love" came on the car stereo to mock him further. As he realised everyone at school would hear about this tomorrow, hot tears began to roll down his pale cheeks.

Chapter 2

Mari

Mr Bad Voice, 1994

Now she was at university, Mari was really hoping that her luck with men would improve. She and Sara were sharing a room together in a student hall at Cardiff University and their social calendar was full to the brim. Obviously, her studying was suffering. Welsh and History were quite coursework heavy and Mari really regretted not going for her preferred course, Film Studies, but her mum and dad had advised her that Film was a bit "flaky" unless she was going to become a movie star (which she wasn't) and that she should stick to some sensible subjects instead. So that's what she'd done and they were exceedingly boring!

In the three months Mari had been a student she'd put on a stone in weight, thanks to the diet of curries and Mad Dog wine booze-ups that they enjoyed in the Students' Union. Mari was in her element with the cosmopolitan environment in Cardiff – a vast contrast to her countrified upbringing in Carmarthenshire. The best thing about being in Cardiff was the vast array of men to choose from. Every colour, every shape, every religion; like the pick-and-mix of mankind.

On her second night, she'd succeeded in pulling the stud of the Halls, Dewi Preece, a third year who delighted in his apparently magical powers over young girls. She hadn't realised at first that he was a sex maniac as he'd shown a great interest in her description of her favourite scene in the new Pulp Fiction movie, as if he might be a fellow film fantatic. His nickname was "The Dog" and as she felt his hands ploughing their way towards her knickers, Mari knew she didn't want to waste her virginity on this greedy creature. "Sorry, but not on the first night," she smiled at him in embarrassment as he lay on her narrow bed, obviously thinking he was God's gift. When he realised that Mari wouldn't change her mind, he left the room in a huff, obviously on a mission to find somebody more eager to "have some fun."

Since then, a few boys had caught her eye. One in particular; Jamie, another fresher in her hall, conformed to her usual type: an artistic loner who played the guitar in a band and who hid his puppy dog eyes beneath a mop-top. She'd tried to have a conversation with Jamie several times, and to be honest, had shown worrying tendencies, following him about on his daily routine for a whole month before Sara had a word with her.

"Mari, everyone's beginning to say you're a stalker. Jamie has no interest in you. He's got a girlfriend at home." The shame she felt listening to Sara's words had shaken her for a while. Uni was such a small island of a world in which everyone knew everybody else's secrets: who was shagging who, who was two-timing who, who was gay, who was "bi".

Mari decided to follow Sara's advice. Sara had enjoyed two relationships already in the short time she'd been at university and knew the score. You had to "act casual" and wait for the object of your affections to come to you. That was the best strategy avoiding shameful rejection and making sure he or she was interested before you moved in for the kill.

On the night she'd first met Nick, she and Sara had been sitting behind their usual table in the Union, sipping their Mad Dog wine and eyeing up the talent. It was a relatively quiet night, a Thursday, so quite a chilled atmosphere with a few drinkers here and there but not too much of a crowd. Some boys were playing pool in the corner – but, as Sara said, it was slim pickings. Apart from one guy… who'd attracted Mari's attention. She hadn't seen him in the Union before – she would have certainly spotted him as he stood out like some exotic bird amongst the crows. He was really tall, 6'5" at least, dark and drop dead gorgeous. All the girls and some of the boys were staring at him. The miracle man, the genetic lottery winner; the perfect face and body. "Have you seen that bloke by the bar?" Mari whispered to Sara. "He's amazing!"

"Out of your league, Mari love," Sara said, using her cigarette as punctuation like Bette Davis in her movies. "And the ones that are that good looking are going to be more trouble than they're worth!"

"What do you mean?" Mari asked, her eyes hooked on the Adonis. His smile was magical, the way he held himself majestic, so different to Jamie and his stupid fringe... This was an example of man at his best, in his prime.

"Well, I went out with that model once, remember?" Sara said.

"What? The one who modelled for that surf shop in Swansea?"

"Gabriel did catalogue work too!" Sara said on the defensive. "Anyway, he was really good looking. Like Action Man he was, every hair in its place but not enough fire in his engine... These overly handsome men don't have to try to have a personality. The packaging is so good, the contents don't matter. I know his type."

"Well, I haven't got a chance anyway but I can dream." Mari smiled over at the Adonis. And to her great surprise, he smiled back at her.

"Another drink?" she asked Sara hopefully. She had to go

up to speak to the vision before another girl grabbed him from under her nose. She'd regret it forever if she didn't seize the opportunity when it presented itself so readily.

"OK. Another Mad Dog please," Sara said.

"OK." Thanking the God of Clothes that she'd worn her new lace mini dress that evening, Mari attempted to sashay seductively to the bar. Before she'd had a chance to initiate a conversation, a mop-topped idiot knocked her arm and spilled a load of beer over her dress!

"Oh, sorry, sorry, I'm so sorry!" The idiot attempted to mop up the mess on her dress with an old hanky.

"Bloody Hell, watch what you're doing!" Mari scowled at him. What a twat, ruining her chances with the Adonis like this!

"Let me buy you a drink, to make up for the… inconvenience," the boy smiled at her in hope. Mari gave him a cursory glance and even though he was quite cute with his moptop and freckles, he wasn't in the same league as the gorgeous guy at the bar.

"No, it's fine, thanks, I don't want to risk any more accidents," Mari said, trying to move closer to the Adonis.

"Oh come on, let me buy you a drink. I'll feel awful if you don't. I'm Owen, I'm a fresher… And you?"

Mari looked at him again and thought his dark brown eyes were indeed quite soulful, perhaps this boy was more her league…. "Mari, and I'll have a G and T please."

The boy grinned and shook her hand, "Mari, lovely to meet you. I'm sorry about messing up your dress."

He really was quite charming Mari thought, as she clocked the dimple in his left cheek when he smiled. "Well you're lucky it's black or I'd send you a dry cleaning bill!" She smiled and pulled out a cigarette. She dropped her lighter on the floor and as she bent down to retrieve it, Owen obviously had the same thought and their heads crashed against each other with a painful thud. "Ouch!"

"Sorry, so sorry, Mari."

Mari's head felt as if it had been bashed by a hammer. "Don't worry about the drink," she said curtly. God, what was wrong with that Owen? He was so clumsy, he was worse than Mr Bean!

She refocused her attentions on the Adonis and still slightly dazed walked away from the dejected looking Owen. Now, how to initiate conversation with the hottie? She'd noticed he was a smoker when she first clocked him. She retrieved her unlit cigarette and popped her lighter in her bag and gently put her hand on his arm. *Ooh!* She could feel his tight muscles under his T-shirt. He was *perfect*! He turned to look at her, his emerald green eyes boring into hers. He was even more breathtaking close-up. She decided to over-turn her new rule of leaving men to make the first move. She snuck a look at Sara but she was busy being chatted up by a long-haired guy.

"Excuse me, do you have a light please?" She smiled her best mega-watt smile. He pulled a lighter from his pocket and lit it for her with a grin. "Thanks," she said. "Now as payment for your courtesy with the lighter, I give you permission to speak to me for a few minutes." This forwardness was a new tactic, but by some amazing miracle, it was working as he followed her obediently to a small table nearby. She looked over with a smirk at Sara, who was staring at her open-mouthed, and put her hand possessively on the Adonis's arm.

"I'm Mari," she smiled, knocking her Mad Dog bottle against his pint glass playfully.

"N-n-ick," he said.

Oh… Oh, no, what was this? Adonis had the weirdest voice she'd ever heard. A voice that was way too deep and made him sound like someone who was really, really slow. His accent wasn't that bad – he was obviously English, not dissimilar to the London accents she heard on *EastEnders* – it was the intonation. It was way too laboured and deliberate. But he'd only said one word, perhaps there was something stuck in his throat. A smidgeon of pork scratching that had gone down the wrong hole perhaps? She tried again. "Well, I haven't seen you around, Nick, where have you been hiding?"

"I've been busy writing my research essay," he smiled at her, caressing her hand gently. Fucking Hell! Typical! He fancied her but he had a really unfortunate voice! Oh well, The Lord giveth and the Lord taketh away. There was no way Nick could have everything and perhaps it was better for her that he wasn't the whole package, or she'd have no chance with him. He was obviously intelligent, the research essay was evidence of that. She decided to get really pissed on Mad Dog so the unfortunate vocal issue wouldn't be a problem. After a few hours in his company, the alcohol had worked its magic and Mari was ready to ignore the tiny voice in her head that was pricking her conscience: "You only fancy him because he's so fit. Not because of his personality which is pretty humdrum and certainly not because of his voice!"

Obviously dying for the goss', Sara came up to their table and put her hand out to Nick, "Hiya. I'm Sara, Mari's best friend."

But before he had a chance to respond, Mari interrupted. "Hi Sar, this is Nick. We're going to go back to his place in town. Are you ok to go home on your own?"

"I'm not on my own, Mari. John's coming home with me."

"Great. See you tomorrow then," Mari said, praying that Sara would take the hint and do one.

"OK. See you tomorrow," Sara said, her eyes narrowing as she decided on her next move. But fortunately, she saw John waiting impatiently for her by the exit and she left without interrogating them further.

"Right, where was I?" Mari flirted. "Oh yes, my favourite film. Well, *Mannequin* of course, a cheesy 80s' classic."

"Oh, I haven't seen Mann-e-quin," Nick said looking deeply into her eyes.

He was lucky he was so damn hot. By concentrating on the visual, Mari could just about ignore the torture of the aural. "Well, I'm sure we can watch it together, some day." Mari smiled at him.

"You ready to go?" Nick asked putting his red-brown leather jacket on. *Oh God, thank you for giving me this Adonis*, Mari prayed happily as they walked out of the Union together. She could see all the girls looking at them as Nick put his arm around her. For once, she'd caught the cream of the crop. And nobody had to know the truth... Well, not for a while anyway. As they both giggled and laughed in Nick's cramped bedroom, Mari started to think of losing her virginity to him – he was certainly attractive enough in the body department. As he kissed her tenderly, she decided to go for it. After all, she was 18 going on 19, and Sara had lost her virginity at 15. Bedding such a stud like Nick would be a feather in her cap to the girls in Halls, maybe even enough to wipe out the memory of the idiot she'd made of herself with Jamie.

Nick undressed her slowly and gently, holding her eyes with his eyes. Oh mygosh, was she really going to do this?

She was ready, wasn't she? And my God, he was so good-looking, she'd be a fool not to! But why did she feel so nervous? Could he hear how loud her heart was beating? Get a grip! Sara'd told her she had nothing to worry about! She tried not to stare as Nick undressed gracefully. Mari almost fainted as she saw the beauty of his body; like David's Michaelangelo, it was flawless. She knew she'd made the right decision about sleeping with him. She'd remember his youthful beauty in her old age, she was sure of that. He kissed her breasts lustfully and stared to speak, until Mari put her hand on his mouth. "We don't need words," she smiled at him, hoping he'd shut his bloody chops and concentrate on the physical…

As Nick snored gently beside her, Mari looked at his small, perfect bottom, like two ripe peaches begging to be squeezed. The sex had been OK, less painful than she'd expected, but it was far from being mindblowing and she didn't think she'd had an orgasm, although she wasn't quite sure how an orgasm was meant to feel, she'd have to ask Sara for some more details on how to actually achieve one. Naturally, she'd have to practice to be perfect.

As she got to know Nick better, the little voice in Mari's head, which she'd been ignoring for weeks, started whispering louder. Sara was delighted with Nick, he was always happy to help her with her Geography homework (he'd got a First in the subject the previous year) and she reckoned that his voice wasn't that much of a problem, "Listen, Mari, you're too much of a perfectionist. His voice is OK. It's not that bad."

"But it's a real turn-off, Sara. Particularly when he's coming – Ma-rry, Ma-rry! Ugh! It makes me cringe!"

"Well, try and keep him for a bit, it's great to have him help me with my essays and the girls still can't believe how you managed to hook such a looker. And he does dote on you."

Yes, Nick did dote on her, but he doted a bit too much. Mari caught him following her to the girls' toilets last week, such was his desire to be in her company at all times.

After two months of dating, she decided that she couldn't ignore the voice in her head any longer. She just didn't like Nick enough to continue with the relationship. And it wasn't just the voice, they didn't really have anything in common. She'd persuaded him to come to a special screening of the Twin Peaks movie with her and he'd just asked stupid questions throughout! Like "Why is the lady speaking to a log?" "Why's the dwarf speaking backwards?" For God's sake! Why had he agreed to come if he wasn't a fan? But still she persevered and continued with the relationship. After all he was really good-looking and as Sara said, her reputation had rocketed amongst her peers, pulling a stunning grad!

But, one evening in the Union, about a week after the *Twin Peaks* debacle, she heard Nick's unfortunate screechy laugh for the hundredth time and a switch clicked on in her head. Enough was enough, particularly as he mentioned them going away on a geological dig together! She hated Geography! Hadn't he twigged that she was an arts person? That she liked films, gigs, music and city breaks? Well, she'd never been on a city break but from what she'd seen of Paris and Venice on the *Holiday Programme*, she knew that would be her cup of tea. Not scrabbling around looking for some volcanic rocks in Pembrokeshire!

After a few stiff G and T's to give her courage, she bit the bullet. "Nick, I'm really sorry. But things aren't going to work out between us. You're lovely…you're gorgeous, but I'm only 18 and I don't want anything too serious. I want to be free, to have options."

"Ma-rry, What are you saying? Do you want to go off with somebody else?"

"Well, no, there's nobody else, but I don't want to be tied down. I've just started university after all." Yes, that was a plausible excuse and a lot kinder than the truth.

His handsome face darkened with anger. "You were just using me. Just for the sex."

"No, not at all."

"I know the type. You're a user Ma-rry!"

Mari could feel her temper rising but she knew she

couldn't tell him the truth. It was too cruel and she didn't want to cause a scene. "I'm really sorry, Nick, but I don't want to mislead you. I'm sure a handsome guy like you will find somebody else, somebody who suits you better."

"That's what my last girlfriend said," Nick mumbled.

"Erm... I'll see you around," Mari said, uncertain of the etiquette involved in dumping a boyfriend – this was her first time. She got up from her chair and left Nick there, staring at her, holding on to his pint like a statue.

She saw Nick a few times after that, with his new girlfriend, a chunky, rosy cheeked second year, who followed him about like a shadow. He completely blanked Mari and all her fresher mates were surprised that she'd done the dumping and not him. But at least she'd lost her virginity and had succeeded in pulling her perfect man, well so far as appearances go, anyway. She'd make sure the next boy had a personality to match.

Owen

Miss One Nighter, 1994

"Owen, my boy, do you realise how lucky we are?" Huw asked as they lolled in Owen's small room in the Halls of Residence.

"What do you mean?" Owen asked as he changed his shirt, ready for another night on the Cardiff tiles.

"We're eighteen, young, free and single. The parents are out of the picture and pretty girls everywhere!"

"Yeah, well, it's ok for you. You've got the gift of the gab," Owen said squeezing a stubborn zit on his chin.

"Yeah, and you're the strong and silent type," Huw said, supping from his can of Stella. "Ying and Yang see. Together we're invincible!"

"Invincible!" Owen scoffed.

"Listen," Huw said. "There are two types of woman. One that likes the charmers, who have advanced verbal and conversation skills, like me. And the other who likes the quiet, brooding types, full of mystery – that's you! We're sorted."

"Where are you reading this?" Owen said. "In *Playboy*?"

"No, *Woman's Own*," Huw replied matter-of-factly. "That's how I know such a lot about women. By reading the magazines they buy, you can learn a lot about their psyches. *Elle*, *Marie Claire*, *Woman's Own*; the keys that open the door to a woman's mind."

"Mum reads *Woman's Own*," said Owen.

"Yeah, well, it's always handy to have an insight into the older woman," Huw smirked. "Just in case…"

"You ready then Huw? Or are you gonna sit here all night like an agony aunt talking crap?" Owen was itching to go to the pub for a pint.

"OK, OK," Huw said, following Owen out of the room.

As they walked down the corridor, Owen clocked a handwritten poster on the wall that was advertising the hall's next film night. "Oh my God, there's a *Twin Peaks* night next week!" Owen beamed; *Twin Peaks* was his favourite TV series.

"God, you've seen it a dozen times and you've got it on video!" Huw puffed impatiently. "There's a limit to watching a weird dwarf speak in riddles you know!"

"Yes, but you spot something new in every viewing..."

"Listen, the only viewing we're going to do tonight, is viewing some fit women. So come on will you!"

The boys walked towards the town centre and Owen felt the usual excitement flowing through his veins. He and Huw had only been at uni for a month and the novelty of going out every night with no curfew was still invigorating. He was so glad that he'd chosen Film Studies for his degree – it was a piece of piss! Consisting mainly of watching films and talking bollocks, it didn't interrupt his quality time in the pub too much. This was freedom, this was youth and Owen was grateful that he had Huw as his partner in crime as he was no good at making new friends and even worse at chatting up girls. Up until now, Huw had managed to pull every night they'd gone out. But Huw didn't have a specific type, his only criteria were they just had to be pretty and ready for fun. Owen hadn't had any luck at all with romance. Yes, he was surrounded by pretty girls at Cardiff Uni, but since the nightmare experience he'd had with Michelle that time, he hadn't been with anyone else and he still hadn't lost his cherry. Every time he fancied a girl, a flashback from that awful night the previous year came back to him in vivid Technicolor and stifled his raging libido.

As if reading Owen's mind, Huw said, "Don't worry, Owen. I'll be your wingman tonight, like Maverick and Goose in *Top Gun*. I've been selfish, copping off without thinking of you and your unfortunate condition." Owen had confided in Huw after the Roath Park incident and Huw wasn't going to let him forget it.

Twenty minutes later they walked into the Students' Union, their favourite drinking hole. After spending their first week drinking like fledgling Oliver Reeds on numerous pub-crawls, they'd voted the Union new local. This was where all the students congregated at the end of the night anyway, so it made sense to get in early to secure a table. As Huw said, if you were hunting (and they were both hunting girls), they needed an "eagle's nest" to to spot the talent from.

"Unfortunate condition?" Owen queried as they both waited by the bar. "Yeah, you know what!" Huw whispered as if he was talking about leprosy. "The small matter of you losing your cherry!"

"Yeah, yeah, there's no need for you to go on about it!" Owen grumbled. "It'll happen when I'm ready. I'm not like you, you're sex mad!"

"That, my funny little friend," Huw said, as he paid the barman, "is because you haven't sampled the pleasures of the flesh to their full potential. Once you do, then it will be like a drug, you have to have more and more…" Huw slurped his pint enthusiastically to emphasise his point.

"OK, I'll take your word for it," Owen said, knowing there was no point answering back as Huw always had the last word.

"Yes, the…unfortunate experience with Michelle has knocked your confidence," Huw said, as he crunched his pork scratchings. "You just need to jump back on the horse again, in case you develop severe psychological issues that could affect your sex life for years to come!"

"More tips from *Woman's Own*? Or is it *Amateur Freud Monthly*, this time?"

"No, *Cosmo*'. Right, look for a pretty girl and go talk to her."

"But what shall I say?" Owen asked, panicking at the very thought.

"Ask her if she'd like a drink, stupid. Look, there's an attractive girl on her way to the bar – over there in that black lacy number."

"A bit out of my league, don't you think?" Owen looked at the girl strutting towards the bar.

"He who dares, Owen bach," Huw said in a fatherly tone. "Now, go up to the bar, keep your cool and ask her if she'd like a drink with you."

Well, he could always pretend to Huw that he'd gone up to speak to her, Owen thought to himself. There was enough of a crowd at the bar to fool even Huw's sharp eyes. He pushed his way through the jostling throng towards the girl. By pretending that he couldn't hear the complaints from the other people waiting at the bar, he succeeded in attracting the barmaid's eye quite quickly. The girl in the lacy dress was stood by his side, impatiently waiting to be served. He took a quick peek at her – yes she was very pretty. Perfect creamy skin, big green eyes and sumptuous breasts… It was a shame he didn't have the balls to start a conversation. He got hold of the two pints of Stella and attempted to carry them in an elegant fashion back to Huw. But as he turned, he felt a jolt to his back as the crowd squeezed closer to the bar. Before he had a chance to take avoiding action, half his pint was all over the pretty girl's lacy frock! *Damn!*

"Oh, sorry, sorry, I'm so sorry, someone pushed me!" Owen said, trying to avoid the temptation of mopping her boobs with his hanky – at least now he'd broken the ice.

"Bloody Hell! watch what you're doing can't you?" The girl scowled at him. Unfortunately, she didn't see the funny side. Oh well, here was his chance to ask her if she wanted a drink. "Let me buy you a drink, to make up for the inconvenience…" Owen smiled appealingly at her, hoping she'd soften.

Bingo! She had! She really was a very pretty girl; he'd always been a sucker for green eyes. And she was a bit Winona-esque in her goth dress... She took a cigarette from her bag; even better, this angel was a smoker! As she dropped her lighter, Owen bent down to retrieve it, hoping to gain some brownie points, but shit, he hadn't realised that she'd bent down to retrieve it as well. God, his head felt like a split melon! This time, his apologies fell on deaf ears and Mari departed, leaving him looking like a right prick. Sadly he watched her walk away; she did have a lovely curvy figure, too... Why was he so hopeless with women?

But then he noticed that she'd started flirting with some enormous big lug who stood head and shoulders above everyone else at the bar. Owen didn't have a hope in hell if that was her type, he thought to himself and made his way back to Huw.

"No joy?" Huw asked. "Don't worry, if her type is some bloody brainless himbo, then that's her problem. I've just spotted two lovelies who'd be perfect for us. They're over there by the juke-box. And this time, I'll come with you, in case you get the urge to tip your drinks over these two as well!"

"They're out of our league, Huw, man," Owen laughed as he looked at the two girls who were very attractive indeed. One had long blonde hair cascading in silken waves down her brown, supple back and a small perfect

54

face like a doll. Whilst the other one had tied back her mass of black curls away from her cute face and was dressed in a short red mini-dress that showed off her lovely figure to perfection. They both wore cowboy boots on their shapely legs. "You know how much I like girls in boots!" Huw's eyes widened. Huw's fetish for women in boots had lead him to take a part time job in the local Clarks shoe shop so he could get closer to pretty girls and their footwear. But unfortunately, the majority of his customers were old hump-backed ladies who wanted help getting sheepskin boots onto the sharp bunion-laden trotters that threatened to escape from their "gravy browning" style support tights. But even this trauma hadn't dampened Huw's passion for boots.

"Out of my league, eh?" Huw scoffed. "Do you think that Warren Beatty would have snared Madonna if he shared your defeatist attitude? Women like confidence, Owen, confidence!"

"Confidence is it? So you're telling me that Madonna fell for Warren Beatty because he's really confident, not because he's loaded and a powerful Hollywood player?"

"Yeah, cos she could have had plenty of that type who are much younger and hotter than Beatty. But he had the X factor see. And that's what I've got. The X factor."

"Well, I haven't."

"Owen, everyone has the X factor, you just need to know how to channel it, that's the trick. Now, watch the master, and you'll see what I mean." Huw got up from his seat and walked towards the jukebox and the girls and Owen followed unwillingly.

The girls were bickering over which song they should put on the jukebox. Huw joined the conversation, "Girls, girls. There's only one song you can possibly choose and don't worry, I have the answer!" The girls turned to look at him in surprise and Huw smiled at them. Owen noticed they were more than happy to listen to him. "Yes, I, like many great thinkers have spent years deliberating over the perfect track-list for a jukebox selection. And after a considerable amount of deliberation amongst the world's foremost thinkers and scientists, there's only one option…" Huw paused, his audience agog.

"Yes?" the blonde asked him, clutching his arm with anticipation. "Leave it to the master, ladies." Huw stood in front of the jukebox and pressed the three magic numbers.

"What did you pick?" the girls squealed?

"'Foxy' by the immortal Hendrix." Huw bowed before them. The girls smiled, happy with Huw's choice. "Now girls, if you want to join me and my friend here, we can share musical secrets and a lot more with you both."

Like a snake-charmer, Huw had succeeded in mesmerising the girls and they followed obediently to the boys' table. "Now, I'm Huw and this is Owen."

"Kerry," the blonde said, shaking Huw's hand. Huw

got hold of her hand and kissed it tenderly. Owen saw Kerry blush with pleasure. Bloody hell, Huw had talent!

"Betsan" the dark haired girl said offering Owen her hand. Owen held her hand sheepishly and gave it a timid shake. He didn't have Huw's confidence but Betsan smiled at him warmly. The night zoomed past with the four enjoying standard drinking games such as Fuzzy Duck and I've Never… Huw always tried to get girls to play, I've Never… It was a simple game. The players would take turns in stating a truth about themselves, for example, "I've never had sex in a lift." And whoever had done that particular deed would have to take a swig of their drink. Of course, Huw had done everything and his glass was empty in ten minutes. Kerry was also quite daring whilst Owen noticed with relief that Betsan, like him, was a lot less extrovert. Huw said I've Never… was a good way of seeing what type of girl you were dealing with – if she was game or not. It was obvious that Kerry was game for most things, but Owen wasn't sure about Betsan. There was a bit of flirting going on but he couldn't be as blatant as Huw, who was already stroking Kerry's legs and kissing her non-stop!

The bell rang for last orders and Huw said to the girls, "Right then, ladies, I'm offering you an invitation that could change your lives – if you're brave enough to accept…"

"Of course we are." Kerry laughed, poking Huw in his ribs.

"Cool. I'd like to extend a warm invitation to you both to come back to my boudoir in Senghennydd Towers to taste the most delicious and knee trembling cocktail in the universe. The 'liver chiller'…"

As the four sat together on Huw's bed, Owen could see that his friend was in his element. He'd hung a glitter-ball on the ceiling, even though Owen had warned him it was girly. Huw had said it was all part of his pulling strategy. To fulfil the same objective, he'd placed a fake fur rug on his bed. "Very tactile, you see," Huw had said, when Owen had made disparaging remarks about it. Huw also had an extensive collection of alcohol and liqueurs in his mini-fridge, a retro cocktail maker and plenty of ice. Marvin Gaye crooned on the stereo and Huw had lit the numerous candles dotted around his room. On the wall, there were tasteful posters of Marilyn Monroe, Brigitte Bardot and Audrey Hepburn. "So the girls think I'm classy," Huw had said knowledgeably. It was like Hugh Hefner's Grotto! This was a room designed to entice girls into staying, not a room which expressed Huw's true personality. It couldn't have been more different to Owen's untidy abode.

It was obvious that the girls felt very at home and were happy downing a number of the "liver chillers" (a secret family recipe Huw said, Pernod and Tia Maria were core ingredients). Owen was holding hands happily with

Betsan and Huw was busy on the bed tickling Kerry, when Betsan whispered in Owen's ear, "I'm ready now."

"Ready for what?" Owen asked.

"Ready for you to ask me back to yours," Betsan leaned towards him and kissed him on his trembling lips. Owen stared at her in shock. She was so pretty; he couldn't believe his luck. Thank God for Huw and his amazing skill with the opposite sex.

"Well, see you tomorrow," Owen said attempting to be cool as he and Betsan got up and left Huw's room. But he had no response from Huw or Kerry, both of whom were too busy snogging to pay any attention to them.

Shit! He should have tidied up a bit, but he couldn't have foreseen this happening!

Owen opened the door with his hands shaking. His room was the polar opposite of Huw's. Posters of his favourite bands hung on the walls; Stone Roses, Nirvana and Bob Marley. The only poster of a girl was his favourite film star, Winona Ryder. He'd fallen for the elfin actress when he saw her in *Heathers,* his favourite movie. There were empty lager cans on the floor and an overflowing ashtray. He kicked the empty cans under the bed and emptied the ashtray quickly. "Sorry, it's not very tidy."

He wondered if Betsan would be interested in hearing him play his acoustic guitar – he'd recently learnt the

Nirvana classic, *About a Girl* which should show his sensitive side, earn a few brownie points and make him look cool to boot. He'd formed a band with some like-minded mates on his course. They'd named themselves Flux Capacitor after the *Back to the Future* gizmo that enabled Marty McFly to go back in time. But before he could strum a note, Betsan made her intentions quite clear and they didn't involve a sing-along.

"Come here you." She was already in the bed and busy undressing beneath the duvet.

Owen hesitated, unsure of first night bedroom etiquette. It also didn't help that he was getting flashbacks to the horrible experience with Michelle in the car – the only proper date he'd had. Shit! He wasn't going to be sick again was he? Nah, nah, he was older and wiser now. He needed to man up. He steeled himself and approached the bed. It was now or never.

"Get your clothes off, then," Betsan said as she flung her bra to the floor. Owen swallowed nervously. The time had come at last… He undressed quickly, not wanting her to change her mind and not wanting it to appear that he was performing some kind of creepy striptease either. Shit! He couldn't get his sock off. He hopped around for a bit, as Betsan struggled to pull the sock off in one go. Finally it snapped off. She giggled. "My God, what are you doing?"

Style it out! He could hear Huw in his head.

"Wouldn't you like to know?" He tried to arch a brow suggestively a là Roger Moore's James Bond and almost jumped out of his skin as her cold hands grabbed his penis... There was no escape now – he was going in!

Owen woke up the next day with his head throbbing painfully. Had it all been a dream? But no he was wedged fast against the wall at the side of his single bed and Betsan's curly head was nestled at his side. He looked at her pretty face fast asleep on his pillow. Huw was right. The sex had been amazing – surprising yet amazing. He'd come a bit too quickly the first time they did it, but Betsan had been very understanding and suggested they go again after a quick ciggie. And indeed, he'd managed to last a whole 5 minutes the second time! God Betsan was perfect... Suddenly, as if she could sense he was watching, she woke up slowly and rubbed her eyes. She looked at Owen for a few seconds before fumbling for her clothes.

"How do you feel?" Owen asked, slightly disappointed that she hadn't greeted him with a good morning kiss. He'd hoped that they might have had another sex session – because he couldn't remember that much from his experience last night – it would be good to do it again, a bit soberer. But he knew it hadn't been a dream, he had "done the dirty" as Huw would put it, when he saw a rather scummy looking condom lying on the floor, next to the bed.

61

"Like shit!" Betsan said as she struggled to get dressed.

"Do you want to go somewhere for coffee?" Owen asked hopefully.

"No, I better not, I feel like crap and I didn't sleep much. I'll come over and see you later when I've had some shuteye."

Kerry and Betsan both lived in another student hall, a stone's throw from Senghennydd Halls and Owen looked forward to staying over in her room as he was sure it must be nicer than his cramped and dark abode. Betsan gave him a quick peck on the cheek before she left the room. Owen smiled to himself. He had a girlfriend at last.

He must have fallen back to sleep as next thing he knew he woke up with a start, feeling something wet on his face. Huw stood there smirking at him, a half-empty glass of water in his hand.

"Well, well. Here he is. Hugh Hefner himself. I take it that we can say mission accomplished?" Huw gestured towards the condom on the floor.

Owen smiled as he dragged himself out of bed. He gingerly picked up the condom and threw it in the bin. He turned to Huw, "She was fantastic."

"Great," Huw said. "Me and Kerry are going to the City Arms for some hair of the dog. Fancy it?"

"No, better not. I'll wait for Betsan, she's coming back later."

"Well, you can leave her a note on the door. You don't want to hang about here all day, do you?"

"I've got a stinking hangover. I can't stomach any more beer!"

"Ok, Gramps. Go back to bed and come down to the pub with Betsan later." Huw sauntered off as fit as a fiddle, without any visible signs of a hangover.

The afternoon dragged on and by 6pm Owen was starting to get restless. He decided to go to the City Arms in case Kerry had told Betsan that she and Huw would be there. He was dying to see Betsan again. He had a quick shower and put on his new shirt and Levis. His hangover was a bit better now and he needed food. Perhaps he could suggest to Betsan that they go for a meal together instead of drinking again. He wanted to last a bit longer this time and see if he could actually give Betsan an orgasm (he wasn't sure exactly how to achieve that but was willing to have a bloody good go.) Of course, he'd woo her properly this time – possibly get some oysters and champagne to enhance the lovemaking?

When he got to the pub, he could see Huw and Kerry cosily ensconced at a table to the left of the door. But to his disappointment, there was no sign of Betsan. Owen went to the bar for a pint and then he spotted her. A couple of tables across from the bar. She was sitting with another bloke! Who was he? Betsan's brother, her friend or what? He walked towards their table with his heart in his stomach. He had to be her brother, he had the same dark curly hair as Betsan. At which point she looked up and saw Owen. He saw her eyes moving shiftily from side to side.

"Hi Betsan."

"Hiya, Owen. This's my boyfriend from back home, Will. Will, Owen's a friend of Kerry's."

"Hiya, mate," Will said casually, before turning back to his pint.

Betsan looked at Owen for a second, before she turned her attention back to Will, her eyes cold.

Owen walked out of the pub, his heart in pieces. Betsan had a boyfriend? Why the hell had she slept with him then? And she must have known her boyfriend was coming up to see her!

"Owen!" He could hear Huw calling, so he slowed down slightly. "Owen, man!" Huw ran up and grabbed his arm. "Listen, mate, I'm really sorry. I didn't know that she had a boyfriend, I swear. Not until Kerry told me today that he'd just turned up out of the blue to surprise her."

"It's OK," Owen said quietly, trying to hide the fact that he was devastated.

"Listen, I'll come round and see you later. Will you be OK?"

"Yes, I'll be fine. Go back to Kerry. It was a one-nighter, that's all," Owen muttered.

"Yeah, that's what college life is all about!" Huw smiled with relief, obviously believing that Owen was fine. "At least you've lost your cherry!" And with a wink, Huw slapped him on the back and pushed back through the door to the City Arms, leaving a waft of beer and fags behind him.

Back in his room Owen lay on his bed. He could still smell Betsan's perfume on his pillow. He'd have to learn not to fall immediately for every girl who showed an interest in him. He had to be more like Huw, a player, not a pathetic drip! He was 18 and he'd proved that he could pull a pretty girl and perform sexually. From now on, he would have relationships for sex and fun but never, ever, again mistake them for love.

Chapter 3

Mari

Mr Sleeze, 2001

Mari sat in a nervous huddle in Reel-Time TV Studios' reception area. She'd reached the shortlist for the position of Assistant Researcher in the Drama Department and she was determined to get it. She'd dressed carefully in a smart pinstriped suit from Topshop and had spent a fortune in Toni and Guy on her hair.

Reel-Time was *the* independent television production company in Cardiff; it received most of the commissions from the big broadcasters and this was a golden opportunity to kickstart her career big style. The nervous young man perspiring by her side was obviously also waiting to be interviewed. She'd noticed his hands shaking as he tried to read a dog-eared copy of *Broadcast*. He looked familiar for some reason. *Oh shit!* She hoped she hadn't had a fling with him in uni. No…she'd remember if she'd slept with him – wouldn't she? The boy had sensed she was looking at him and lifted his head to look at her.

"You going for the Drama job?" Mari asked. Well, she might as well assess the competition. And he was quite cute with his freckles and wide dark eyes. Although his curly hair was a bit unruly and in dire need of a good brush!

"Erm…yes. I'm a nervous wreck!" He gave her a shy smile and she noticed the dimple in his left cheek. Yes, he was a bit of a cutie, but she couldn't be distracted now, he was the enemy!

"Is this your first job?" Mari asked.

"Yes, just finished the Chance media training course," he said quietly. "And you?"

"Yes," Mari answered. "Trying to be a student for as long as possible," she laughed. Then her attention was drawn to another man, who came to sit by her side. God, he was stunning! She hoped he wasn't going for the job too! He wore an expensive designer suit and must have been pushing thirty. He was a dead ringer for Johnny Depp, she thought as she eyed him surreptitiously…

"Got a job interview?" the man asked her, grinning sympathetically at Mari.

"Yes. Is it obvious?"

"Well, you do look like a lamb going to slaughter," the man laughed, displaying perfect pearly white teeth.

"Don't say you're going for the same job!" Mari knew she wouldn't have a hope in hell if he was in the running.

"No, I'm here to meet with the big boss. I'm the company's solicitor," he said. "Robert, Robert Jones."

"Mari, Mari Roberts," Mari replied, feeling as if she was introducing herself on a quiz show.

"Well, Mari," the man said quietly in her ear. "If you fancy discussing how your interview went over a drink, later, give me a ring," he pressed his business card into her shaky hand.

Wow! He obviously didn't believe in hanging about. The receptionist called her name for interview and Mari smiled at Robert who crossed his fingers for her as she followed the receptionist out into the corridor. Her new suit and hair had been worth every penny job or not!

Mari didn't get the job and, to be honest, she was quite relieved as judging from the interview experience everyone seemed in awe of the Drama boss, who seemed to rule the roost like some Joan Collins character from an 80s' soap. The woman who interviewed her was an insipid character, the "Deputy Head of Drama" and kept referring to this "Maggie" woman throughout the interview. "Maggie believes that realism is the key to 20th century Drama…When Maggie visited L.A. recently" and so on and so on. It probably hadn't helped that Mari had mistakenly confessed to not watching any of the crappy programmes the Queen Bitch's production company had made for S4C in recent years. But was that such a deal-breaker? Why would she want to watch some North Walians squabbling in a clothes shop? Anyway, it was obviously a lucky escape, she hadn't got good vibes from the place. But she had acquired something even better – a cool and sophisticated boyfriend: Robert.

Tonight would be their third date and Mari looked at her reflection in her bedroom mirror for the hundredth time. The leopard print mini dress had seemed like a good idea in the shop but now she wasn't so sure.

"Do you think it's too short?" she asked Sara, who was lying on Mari's bed reading *Cosmo*.

"You've got the legs to carry it off and Robert will love it!" Sara laughed.

"Yes, but I don't want him to think that I—"

"What, wear a mini dress occasionally? Listen, you've been out with him three times, you know what comes next!"

"Well, I'm not sure if I'm ready."

"You don't need to rush do you, but if you want to create an impression, well, that frock is a great way of going about it!"

"Right, I knew it was too short!" Mari took the dress off dropping it over the back of an already loaded chair. I shouldn't wear it if I don't feel comfortable. I'm going to wear my black lace dress. It's nice but not too tarty."

"OK, but get a move on, it's a quarter to seven!"

Mari felt much more comfortable in her black dress. If this dress could have talked, it would have had a wealth of interesting stories to share. It had been a faithful companion on numerous nights out over the last two years. It showed off her cleavage without being tacky and since Robert was very classy she didn't want him to think she was cheap.

Robert. She couldn't believe she'd managed to pull such a looker. Since their first coffee together, they'd met up twice. On both occasions, Robert had been the perfect gentleman, apart from one or two red-hot snogs, he hadn't made any sleazy overtures, but she knew tonight was the night... Thanks to a few disastrous one-night flings in her very early twenties, Mari had selected the second month of dating as the ideal time to start a sexual relationship. By then, you'd learnt enough about the man to know if he was a dud or a stud. And Robert was very promising. Tonight she was going over to his flat in the Bay and he was cooking. It wouldn't be pizza and ice-cream if she'd judged things right. Robert was almost too good to be true; he was single, 28 years old, a solicitor for a successful company in town... Yes, he had everything including a great sense of humour, jaw-dropping looks and excellent taste in film and music. For their first date, he'd managed to get tickets for them to see the Super Furry Animals in Bristol! But was she ready to have sex with him? The fact she'd put a pack of condoms in her handbag suggested that she was ready. To be honest, she'd dreamt of having sex with Robert since their first meeting.

The taxi stopped outside a stylish block of flats in Cardiff Bay. Robert, naturally, lived in the penthouse on the top floor. God, he should be out of her league. She and Sara and their mate Helen, whom they met in their last year in uni, still lived in a poky terraced house in Roath – more piss-house than penthouse! But as long as she could get her own house before she was 30, she'd be OK and she was only 24 now. She felt a shiver of excitement as she walked towards the door and looked for his name by the entryphone. She hadn't been to the lion's den before, but she knew, the flat, like its owner would be flawless…

"Mari…" Robert smiled at her as he opened his apartment door. He looked amazing. He wore a dark navy t-shirt and Diesel jeans. Mari was pleased she'd gone for the black dress. She'd have looked like a real slapper if she'd worn the leopard print number. She followed Robert into the flat and tried not to stare too much. Yes, as she'd expected, it was luxurious and expensive: black minimalist furniture in the living room and abstract art hanging on the plain white walls, and a huge widescreen TV sitting emperor-like in the far corner of the room. It was obvious that Robert was loaded. He'd lit some candles on a small dining table, which had been laid out as if they were in a 5-star restaurant.

"I'll take your coat," Robert said and she handed it to him with a smile. "Did you find the flat OK?" he asked from the kitchen as he poured them both a glass of wine.

"Yes, the taxi driver knew the place. This is a lovely flat, Robert."

"Thank you. Well, to be honest, I got the cleaners in today to make sure everything was perfect for you." Mari smiled thanking the sweet Lord that Robert couldn't see the state of her bedroom. Thanks to her mum having been fanatical about cleaning, Mari's attitude towards housework was relaxed to say the least. Robert brought two glasses of white and sat on the black leather sofa beside Mari. Billie Holiday was singing the blues on the stereo and Mari had a handsome man, a good glass of wine and a lovely evening ahead of her. She'd really struck the jackpot with Robert – he was perfect! There were butterflies in her tummy and she wondered if this was love.

"You look gorgeous," Robert smiled, taking her glass of wine, putting it on the coffee table and leaning in...

His kisses made her shiver with longing. She started to hope the supper would be over and done with quickly!

As if he'd read her mind, Robert said, "You have to forgive me, I don't cook that much these days, but I've got oysters to start, then risotto and for afters... I hope you like tiramisu."

"My favourite dessert..." Mari smiled, knowing that she would only eat a tiny portion as she didn't want to be too full to be passionate!

The food, like Robert, was perfect. He treated her like a queen; filling her glass constantly and praising her to the skies. Being in the company of a sophisticated, successful and handsome man was like a breath of fresh air.

"What do you really want from a relationship, Mari?" Robert asked her as she tucked into her tiramisu with gusto, her previous resolution forgotten when confronted with the silky, chocolatey dream pud. Mari looked at his penetrating dark eyes before answering him. She could hear Sara's warning voice in her head, "Don't mention marriage and settling down for God's sake, or he'll make like the Road Runner: out of there!"

"Well, I want to share my time with someone who can teach me something about life, someone I love to spend time with…" *And someone who looks like Johnny Depp and who thinks I'm fucking fantastic,* the little voice in her head whispered.

"Well, we're birds of a feather then, Mari," Robert said with a blinding smile. "It's so hard to find someone on the same wavelength these days. You'd be surprised how many girls are scary bunny boilers, or even worse, gold diggers!"

Mari laughed with him although she felt a pinprick of guilt as she heard him talking about money. She had to admit that Robert's standard of living was very attractive to her, as she usually, pulled "Church mice" as her mother called them. Yes, the artistic shiftless types without a penny in their pockets who expected her to look after them. But for once, it seemed, she'd hit the jackpot.

"I don't want to be a trophy wife living off her husband's cash. I want to make something of myself and earn my own money."

"Could you be more perfect?" Robert sighed as he pulled out her dining chair and guided her towards the sofa, his hand slowly slipping from her waist to the bottom of her dress zip. He opened a bottle of champagne and poured the golden bubbles into her glass. "To you and me – kindred spirits."

"Kindred spirits," Mari echoed, feeling as if she'd been hypnotised, such was the strength of her attraction to him.

"Right, time for an old classic," Robert said, putting a new CD on the stereo. Doris Day's lilting voice started to sing, "Move over Darling".

"Would you like to dance, madam?"

Mari got up and surrendered to his arms. Robert was exactly like her – he loved retro music. As their lips met, she felt as if she was in a 50s' romance, starring Cary Grant as Robert. She, of course, would be played by Grace Kelly, who else? The song came to an end and Robert said lightly, "Right, how about a film and a nightcap?"

Mari agreed enthusiastically, even though she couldn't

wait to go to bed with him; she was such a film fanatic, she was happy to watch one of Hitchock's classics before the big moment. Hitchcock was his favourite auteur he'd told her on their first date. They returned to the sofa and Robert switched the video on. Mari settled down and put her head on his shoulder. The credits appeared on the screen: "Foxy Productions" followed by the title, *Orifice Management.*

What the hell? She stared at Robert in shock and saw his black eyes were fixed on the big TV screen. As if hypnotised, Mari stared at the screen, hoping vainly that *Orifice Management* was a badly titled straight to DVD rom com. But when the first scene started to play her worst fears were realised. This wasn't a Hitchcock movie, it was a cock movie! A crude porno set in an office. And worst of all, a cheap badly made porno, with the main character a rosy cheeked, portly bloke with a big black 'tache, furry sideburns and an obvious wig on his head. He wore a business suit that looked like he was about to burst out of it any second. His penis was obviously hard and straining to escape from his tight trousers. Next a Page 3 type walked in to the room. Dressed up as a secretary, she looked quite innocuous apart from the fact her bra was hanging out of her blouse and she had lots of fake tan on her face. She wore black spectacles to signify her calling and her peroxide hair was tied in a bun. "Take this down, Miss Jones," the main man said in a faux American accent. "Certainly, sir," the girl replied as she started to give the man a blow job. He pulled at her hair until her bun fell in blonde waves on her back.

A few excruciating minutes went by as Mari pondered her next move. The scene was as sexy as a kid's funeral! *Ugh!* Now the girl was completely naked, her sad little breasts bouncing in the air as the moustachioed monster took her from behind. She took a peek at Robert and saw he was obviously aroused. He'd started to breathe heavily too! Shit! And she'd thought he was perfect in every way. She turned back to the screen again. Was she the problem? Was she too provincial? Too puritanical? After all, millions of people enjoyed completely normal and natural sex lives and watched porn regularly – well, Sara and her boyfriend, Tom, did as Sara enjoyed telling Mari. But as the film unfolded, with an additional girl and another bloke, with the biggest penis she'd ever seen outside a stable, joining in the fun, Mari was sure this wasn't her cup of tea.

"Erm, Robert…"

"Mmm?" Robert said, tickling her arm lightly with his eyes still fixed on the screen.

"Sorry to be so square, but, well, I don't really like porn films."

"What?" Robert turned towards her in surprise. "Everyone likes films. Even the girls who say they don't!"

"Porn just doesn't do it for me… If they were good

looking it'd be something…" Mari had enjoyed near orgasmic experiences watching Brad Pitt, for example, showing off his ample talents as the sexy cowboy in *Thelma and Louise*, and had had several erotic dreams about Gary Oldman's Dracula coming into her room on a moonlit night (as a young man of course, not the horrible old bloodsucker). But porno characters who resembled refugees from a seventies sitcom, old cocks and ropey tits everywhere, didn't push her buttons.

"Well, I've got loads more!" Robert said brightly, obviously thinking it was this film in particular and not the genre of film that was to blame. He opened an innocent looking cupboard beneath the stereo and Mari saw a scarily huge collection of videos.

"How's about *Hannah Does Her Sisters*, or *The Loin King*, or look, how about *Bedman and Throbbin*? There's loads of fit men in that one!"

"It just doesn't do it for me, sorry," Mari said, not able to look him in the eye.

"Fair enough," Robert said abruptly, switching the TV off and putting the stereo back on. But Doris Day had lost her lustre. Robert bent down to kiss her and even though she kissed him back Mari knew she wouldn't be joining him in the bedroom tonight or any other night. How could she make a swift exit whilst leaving Robert with his dignity and ego intact…?

"Come here," Robert said huskily, grabbing her hand

and putting it on his crotch. His penis was hard like iron. Now, Mari was completely lost. What was she meant to do? Whatever it was, she didn't fancy recreating one of the scenes from *Orifice Management* so she said quietly, "I'm sorry, Robert, but I think I'd better go now, I have work in the morning." She moved her hand away from him carefully, as if he had a venomous snake in his trousers.

"What?" Robert laughed coldly. "You playing hard to get or what? You've been begging for it all night with those puppy dog eyes! What's changed?"

Mari got up from the sofa and reached for her bag. "Thanks for the dinner, but I'm sorry, I've got work in the morning."

"You're a real prick-teaser you know?" Robert said sharply. "You're lucky that I'm a gentleman. You could get into real trouble behaving like this!"

Mari's hackles rose at this. "What? You think any woman with a bit of sense would want sex after watching the cast of Hi-de-Hi shagging each other up the arse? I thought we were sharing dinner, not *Orifice Management!*"

"Frigid, that's your problem, Mari!" Robert shouted.

"Well, we'll have to agree to disagree, Robert. Now if I could have my coat, I'll be on my way."

Robert went to fetch her coat, his face as miserable as a bulldog's arse.

"Thanks," Mari said sarcastically as he threw her coat at her. "Enjoy your smutty films, saddo!" she added, slamming the door behind her.

As she related the tale to Sara and Helen, she was dismayed to see both her friends in fits of laughter.

"Why are you laughing?" Mari asked angrily. "My love life is a complete disaster!"

"Oh, Mari," Helen laughed. "Only you could have these adventures! *Bedman and Throbbin!*"

They were both in stitches again. "And *Hannah Does her Sisters*!" Sara added, snorting with laughter on the sofa.

"OK, OK," Mari said, a smile starting to spread across her face. "It's a funny story to recite back one day, but not yet, OK?" The girls nodded soberly as they tried to stop laughing.

"Right, then Mari," Helen said, in a motherly tone. "How's about a nice cup of tea and a chick-flick?"

"OK," Mari said, settling down on the sofa obediently.

"Yes," Helen said winking at Sara. "I went to BlockBusters earlier and they had a movie I've been waiting ages to see…"

"Oh, yeah?" Mari said disinterestedly.

"Yes," Sara said. "I knew you'd love it… *Saturday Night Beaver*!" Once again her two friends were doubled up with laughter.

"Thanks a lot, for your support girls!" Mari chided, even though she wanted to laugh too.

"Well, you've learnt another valuable lesson, Mari," Sara said, matter of factly, after she'd recovered from her laughing fit.

"What's that? Not to trust any bloke, because they're all freaks?" Mari wisecracked.

"Not exactly," Sara said. "I think the most apt saying is, 'Never judge a book by its cover...' And let's be honest, you liked the pigsty more than the pig..."

"Yes and what a pig he turned out to be!" Mari added and the three girls started to laugh and laugh until the tears were streaming down their cheeks.

Mari didn't see Robert for a few months, but then she spotted him out one Saturday night. He was as suave looking as ever in his expensive suit, chatting happily to a young girl who looked like she'd just received a free ticket to heaven. Mari knew it would be just a matter of time before Robert showed *Beverly Hills Cock* for the poor cow's entertainment. She just hoped, for his sake, that his new conquest would share the same taste in movies...

Owen

Mrs Robinson, 2001

Owen sat in the reception area with his nerves in shreds. It was a miracle that he'd actually reached Reel-Time's shortlist, considering the bullshit he'd manufactured for his application form. He'd pretended that his favourite film was *La Dolce Vita* (and not *Night of the Living Dead*) and had stated that he always watched S4C programmes (and not just the rugby). Hopefully, they wouldn't quiz him too much about S4C's dramatic output – he was hoping some superficial waffle would be enough for him to get through this ordeal. He had to get a job soon – he couldn't leech off his mum and dad for ever – soon they'd insist on him going into teacher training so he could have a "steady profession", like Huw, who was now a "respectable" Welsh teacher in a local high school. No, he couldn't be doing with dealing with stroppy kids and jobsworth headmasters. This job would suit him down to the ground. It was in the media, he would be reading scripts and hopefully might get to make a programme or two eventually. But there was bound to be some stiff competition as these low level jobs for beginners were as rare as hen's teeth.

He'd clocked the attractive girl sat by his side immediately. She was obviously waiting to be interviewed, too. She looked very sure of herself in her smart suit and she had a leather briefcase! *Shit!* Why hadn't he brought his briefcase? After all, his grandma had spent a fortune on it as his graduation present. But it was too late now.

He noticed the girl was watching him so he raised his head from the magazine he'd been pretending to read for the last 10 minutes. As he looked more closely at her pretty face, a strange feeling of déjà-vu came over him. Had he met her before? She reminded him of someone…

"You going for the Drama job?" she asked him.

"Erm… yes, I'm a nervous wreck!" Well, he might as well respond, she'd started the conversation, she might be up for a minor flirt – just to forget the nerves. As she quizzed him further, he felt himself blush. He could smell her lovely perfume and her wide green eyes were, well, mesmerising. God, she was sexy… Then just before he had a chance to ask her out for a drink after the interview, to compare notes, this yuppie bastard had to come and spoil everything! Fucking Hell! Typical, and he'd been doing quite well conversation-wise. But no, she and the yuppie were whispering cosily to each other and she'd obviously forgotten about Owen. He returned to his magazine. Why were girls so shallow?

The following day, to his great surprise, Owen learnt that he'd actually got the job. And here he was again, waiting in the reception area. But this time, he'd be meeting his new boss, the Head of Drama, Maggie Lewis. What kind of woman would she be, he pondered. Motherly? Kind? Or a bulldog in a Chanel suit…?

"Owen?" a female voice broke his reverie. He raised his head and saw a sophisticated and attractive woman in her early forties smiling at him.

"Yes, hello, hi," he said, dropping the magazine he'd been pretending to read for the last twenty minutes. He bent down to pick it up but as he got up quickly, he felt something rip from the abrupt movement. Shit! Could things get worse? He thanked the Lord that he had his jacket on too. Now, he'd have to sweat all day, lest he reveal that, like some wimpy version of the Incredible Hulk, he'd burst out of his trendy shirt.

"Come with me, Owen," the woman said. Owen followed her sheep-like as she strutted through reception. Owen noticed the towering stilettos on her feet – they were red, shiny and sharp… Huw would have been in his element as his fetish for boots had faded in favour of sexy stilettos. His new boss had long shapely legs and the body of a model. She scared him shitless already! Opening the door to a large corner office on the top floor, she ushered him in. Owen looked around. There was a huge desk and two expensive looking leather chairs. Various papers and scripts were piled on the table and posters of past productions were hanging on the walls. The award winning drama *Hidden*, about a gay love-affair between a German Prisoner of War and an RAF Officer; the Welsh kitchen sink drama *Family*, which was still offering a pension to cast-offs from the nightly soap-opera, *Pobol y Cwm*; a pop quiz for kids, *Disk*, and the hit show for toddlers *Teaching Teddy*…there was a wealth of TV history here. And he could be part of it!

"Owen, take a seat," Maggie said warmly. "I'm Maggie Lewis. Now, have you been offered a coffee?"

"Erm, no…"

"Oh dear. Well, we'll have a cup of coffee together now and I'll explain your role in the Reel-Time family," she smiled at him with her blood-red lipstick shining against her snow-white teeth. She picked up the phone: "Two coffees, now."

Wow that was a bit sharp. Yes, she was attractive, but she was also very powerful. Her jet black hair was styled in a sleek tight bob, like Louise Brooks in the old black and white movies in the 1920s. Her eyes were green like a snake's and she had a striking beauty spot on her left cheek, like Liz Taylor in *Cleopatra*.

"As you know," she said, "I'm the Head of Drama here and you'll be working on my team. Recently I've been working on our new drama series for young people, *Scallies*, in North Wales. Perhaps you saw the last series?" She fired the question like a bullet from a gun.

Yes, Owen recalled, he had been unfortunate enough to watch one episode of *Scallies*, which had consisted of

84

following about a crew of young people who worked in a clothes shop in Caernarfon and spent most of their time arguing and shagging. He feigned enthusiasm and said brightly, "Yes, it was great, erm…a breath of fresh air."

"Well, we had a lot of script problems but now we have a new head writer and I'm confident the second series will be much more successful."

Second series? God! How the hell did such rubbish manage to get a second series?

As if she'd read his mind, Maggie said nonchalantly, "We're lucky that our productions for S4C all get to the second series, that's the norm now. It's cheaper to cut a deal and pay for two series at once these days."

Owen nodded his head wisely as if he understood what she was talking about. The surly girl from reception walked in with their coffee, but this time, she was smiling broadly.

"Well, Owen," Maggie said, as she sipped her coffee, "as you can see from my desk, I have a stack of scripts that I haven't had time to read. Most of them are going to be utter crap, but they have to be read, reports have to be written and a decision made as to whether they have any potential for development. And that's where you come in."

"Oh?" Owen asked, tipping some hot coffee on his suede jacket.

"Yes. If you think a script has potential, you will write

a more detailed report for me. Content, character breakdowns, story, which broadcaster we should target and so forth. As for the shit ones, well, a polite letter of rejection will suffice."

"Fine, no problem," Owen said, feeling more lost than ever. How was he supposed to know if something was any good? What if he rubbished a brilliant script that turned out to be a BAFTA sweeping success for a rival company? After all, his tastes were mainly sci-fi and horror and a smattering of comedy. What if he turned down the next *Office*?

"Grab a box of scripts and I'll ask Linda to set up a desk for you," Maggie said plonking a heavy box in his shaking arms and leading him out of the office. She smiled at him as she ushered him to a desk where a rosy cheeked and obviously busy girl was waiting for him.

"I'm sure you'll make a valuable addition to the team, Owen," she said smoothly, patting his arm with her small white hand. Owen noticed that her long red talons paused for a few seconds on his bicep, before she returned to her office.

Owen settled down quickly to the 9-5 life. He learned from other team members that Maggie always gave the newbie the "script reading challenge" so she could grasp any strengths or weaknesses her new protégé might have. If the script reports were unsatisfactory, then the newbie would be disposed of smartly following the three-month trial period. Owen also learnt that everyone in the office lived in fear of Maggie. When she was out of the building the pressurised atmosphere was transformed, with personal phone calls and general timewasting on the internet taking over. But he didn't dare do any slacking. He was determined to pass his trial period and secure his place as the new hot researcher in the Reel-Time family. About two months after he started the job, he received an email from Maggie inviting him to a development meeting in her office at 6pm. This wasn't unusual, several staff members usually stayed behind after work to discuss new projects with "Madame" as they'd sneakily nicknamed their boss. But to invite a lowly assistant researcher was almost unheard of.

"Perhaps you're in for the high-jump," his colleague Linda teased. "She usually only calls assistants in after work to give them a bollocking!"

Owen's heart sank to his shoes. *Fuck!* And he'd been working so hard, what more did the bitch want? Blood? For once, and to his extreme discomfort, the hours zoomed by. As it was a Friday, all of his co-workers had buggered off by 5.30pm (following the POETS ethos – Piss Off Early Tomorrow's Saturday) and he was the only one in the office. He'd already packed the stuff from his desk drawer so he could make a dignified exit if the worst happened. At 6pm sharp, he knocked on Maggie's door.

"Come in!" she commanded. He walked into her office with his hands shaking. "Owen." Maggie smiled. "Take a seat." Owen sat at the edge of his chair, ready to up and leave as soon as the command was given. "Listen," Maggie said, "I've called you in to compliment you on the good work you've been doing. Your reports are concise, well-written, packed with information and you've got strong creative skills. In time, you'll make a great little producer."

Owen glowed at this unexpected praise and smiled, "Thanks very much Mad— Maggie." He'd almost ballsed it up and called her Madame by mistake.

"And to celebrate, I want you to work closely with me on a new project." Maggie smiled, leaning back in her chair. "I'm preparing a new series for BBC Wales – they've asked for a new sexy sci-fi series and that's what they're going to get. Now, I know it's Friday night and I'm sure a young man such as yourself has made arrangements for the evening…"

"Oh, no, I haven't got any plans," Owen said, even though Huw and he had arranged to go out for a few beers. Sci-fi! He would be in his element – he'd worshipped at the altar of *X-Files* and *Dr Who* since his youth. Perhaps this would be his big break. It might even lead to him being a sci-fi movie director in the long run, particularly if it was in English where he could appeal to a larger audience – he could shoot teaser trailers to go online!

"Great," Maggie said contentedly. "Now let me explain to you how I see this series developing…"

Two hours later, Owen had written a page full of notes. Maggie smiled at him and said, "Listen, I'm starving. Do you fancy a bite to eat somewhere? You deserve a treat after working so hard."

"Yes, that'd be great," Owen said, not really sure of the protocol but knowing he couldn't very well turn down her offer. His night out with Huw would have to wait an hour or two more. They left the Reel-Time building together and Owen felt very adult as he climbed into Maggie's stunning gold Porsche Boxter. This was the life! A fantastic boss who could see his potential and who was taking him out to dinner… Maggie drove to an upmarket brasserie restaurant in Cardiff Bay. The five star eatery was way too pricey for Owen's pocket, but thankfully, he'd bought his credit card. He selected the cheapest option from the menu at first, but Maggie encouraged him: "Owen, you can have anything you want, I'm paying tonight." He smiled awkwardly and after some deliberation selected fillet steak with all the trimmings. *Well, if she insisted…* After he'd calmed down a bit, and with the help of a very fine glass of red, he started to enjoy Maggie's company. She laughed at all his jokes and was much more laidback than she had been while they were working. He almost forgot that this was the same Madame who put the fear of God into everyone between nine and five. By the time the bill had arrived and he'd stuffed steak, crème brulee and enough wine to sink the Titanic down his gullet, Owen felt very contented indeed, almost relaxed. Maggie was fantastic and she was also very sexy in the right light, he realised, noting her ample breasts pushing forward against taut blouse buttons as she leant towards him.

"Well, then Owen. How about it? Back to my place for some champers and...fun?"

"*Fun?* What did she mean? No, she didn't... Did she? Had he actually managed to pull a clever, sophisticated, sexy woman like Maggie? His boss? And without even trying? *Shit!* What was he meant to do? The wine he'd consumed had turned his brains to candyfloss. She probably only meant a night-cap. She didn't want sex with him, did she? She was almost old enough to be his mother! Or at least his mother's younger sister. He followed Maggie obediently to the car park and climbed into the plush comfort of the Porsche. His head was spinning. What the hell was she planning to do with him now? Discuss the new sci-fi project in more detail perhaps? She was undeniably attractive. He noticed her long athletic legs and the rather generous cleavage she was displaying as she drove the Porsche around Cardiff Bay. But oh my god, could he handle such a powerful woman? She'd eat him alive! And she was his boss!

Maggie made a tidy job of parking the Porsche

outside a huge Georgian house in Penarth – the seaside mecca, a stone's throw from Cardiff city centre and full of huge grandiose houses, that no one, except for the genuinely minted could afford. She opened the door and smiled at him as she yanked him in roughly by his lapels. *What the fuck—?* The door slammed shut and Maggie pushed him Owen against the wall at the foot of the stairs and started kissing him passionately. Owen kissed her back eagerly, still doubting that this was actually happening, imagining that it was just a particularly lucid hallucination of some kind and he would soon wake up in his pokey single bed, with Huw's loud snoring echoing through the bedroom wall. But no, this was real, he felt Maggie's tongue pushing into his mouth… She kicked off her heels and Owen realised that she was quite short – around 5'4" to his 6 feet. She wasn't that scary, or was she? He could smell the booze on her breath and she was a bit unsteady on her feet – he didn't want to take advantage. He pulled back from her embrace and looked down at her. He didn't want the sack the next day for jumping the boss. "Maggie, are you sure we should be doing this?"

"Owen," Maggie said smiling. "I may be tipsy, but I know what I'm doing. I've never had sex with a staff member before. But you're different. I can't stop thinking about you. You're so gorgeous and innocent… I have to have you!" With this, she grabbed his hand and led him to her bedroom. Owen barely had time to clock the antique oak furniture and sumptuous linen bedding before she pulled him hard on to the bed. Owen obeyed, hardly believing his luck. Huw would be so jealous when he heard about this little escapade!

Owen had always fantasised about having sex with an older, more experienced woman, who knew exactly what she was doing in bed, yes, his own Mrs Robinson, and it had come true! Maggie was like a wildcat between the linen sheets. All teeth and sharp nails, her tight, curvaceous body as supple as a girl half her age. Owen was like putty in her hands as she caressed him and drove him crazy with her skilled lovemaking. He felt himself coming like a train as she rode him relentlessly. He couldn't believe he was having sex with the boss, his hands buried deep in her white sumptuous bosom. He yelled out, "Madame!" as he reached orgasm.

Maggie laughed as she continued to ride him hard. "And again, my love," she whispered in his ear as she continued to grind against him, his penis locked deep inside her. Things didn't get much better than this...

After two hours of intensive love making, Maggie was obviously satisfied as they both shared the clichéd post-coital cigarette together.

"You are such a sexy boy," she purred as she stroked his chest hair with her long talons.

Owen wasn't sure how to react to this but returned the compliment, "And you are a very sexy lady…"

Maggie ground the cigarette in an ashtray and got out of bed. Owen did his best not to look at her lovely body, but couldn't help peeking at her shapely bottom.

"I'm just going to have a shower," she said tying her silk robe around her. "Listen, I've got an early meeting tomorrow morning, so I hope you don't mind that we call it a night now. I've got some money for a taxi if you need it…"

Owen felt a bit crestfallen at this. Was she chucking him out already? Did he not make the grade? As if she'd read his mind she leaned over him and kissed him fully on the lips. "If I don't send you home now, I'll just want to fuck you all night," she grinned. "I need my wits about me tomorrow; we've got a big pitch to do at the BBC."

Owen smiled with relief and kissed her back. "Good, I thought I hadn't satisfied you." God, why did he use the word "satisfied" – he sounded like rent-a-stud or something!

"I'm more than satisfied… Oh God, I can't help it, once more, but then you'll have to go," she admonished as she jumped back into bed and into his arms. God, he really fancied her; he really hoped she'd want to do this again…

"And where have you been all night?" Huw asked as Owen tip-toed into the living room of their tiny flat like a giddy

Jane Austen debutante returning from the ball. It was two in the morning and there were empty beer cans a full ashtray and a heap of PSP paraphernalia on the floor. He was still annoyed that Owen hadn't come home earlier as arranged.

"Listen!" Owen said, still shaking from the excitement and bliss of sharing Maggie's bed. "You'll never believe it. I slept with my boss...!"

"What?" Huw shouted, jumping from his chair in shock. "You slept with Madame? How on earth did you manage that?"

"I don't know," Owen said smugly, sitting down on the sofa and helping himself to a can of beer. "She asked me to come to her office after work, told me she was very happy with my performance and asked me to work with her on a big new sci-fi project. Then we went out for a meal and then back to her place and...well..."

"Fucking hell!" Huw sighed as he lit a cigarette. "How was the sex? Was it good?"

"Mind blowing"

"Well, naturally," Huw said. "A mature woman with her experience... You, my jammy little friend have trapped yourself a cougar!"

"Cougar?"

"Yes, a new breed of well-preserved mature lady, which targets young men like us for...extra-curricular activities," Huw said with a surprised smile on his face. "I thought it was a myth...until now."

"She was amazing," Owen said, transported. "Like a wild animal, I've never, ever, come like that before."

"OK, OK, no need to rub it in," Huw said, throwing a cushion at him. "Some of us have been sitting here all night like muggins waiting for you to come home!"

"Sorry, mate, we'll go out tomorrow night," Owen promised, downing the rest of the beer from his can.

"Do you think she'll come back for more?" Huw asked. "Ah! And how will things be in work on Monday?"

Shit! What if everyone in work found out about their liaison? The gossip would be unbearable. And worst of all, would Maggie get pissed off and sack him? "What should I do, Huw?"

"Nothing at all. Let her make the first move. After all, she is the boss…"

Owen was quaking in his Hush Puppies on Monday morning as he sat at his desk. What if Maggie regretted their night of passion and sacked him on the spot? How could he have done such a thing? "Never shit on your own doorstep," that was one of the golden rules – for anything. And he'd just done the biggest dump in the history of humanity! He opened his email. And there he saw it, "Maggie@reeltime.com" He opened the email with his hands shaking. The message was plain and simple:

Dear Owen

Many thanks for your input on Friday. It was a very satisfactory meeting. I hope you are available for more development work tonight. 16 Windsor Road, Penarth, 8pm.

Best wishes, M

Phew! He wasn't about to get sacked! And if he was reading this right, she wanted another sex session... He wasn't sure he had the energy to do this every night! God knows – he'd been knackered all weekend. He smiled to himself as he saw her coming out of her office. He caught her eye and she smiled at him flicking her tongue quickly over her lips. Blushing, Owen turned back to his computer. A secret like this was an amazing turn-on. He felt as if he was on telly not researching it.

After two months of clandestine meetings and red-hot sex, including some provocative moments on Maggie's desk during late night development sessions, Owen started to feel like he was in a horror movie rather than *Secretary*. The "extra-curricular" attention he'd enjoyed so much when his relationship with Maggie had begun had quickly waned. She wanted him to come back to her place almost every night and even though the sex was amazing, Owen missed lazy nights in front of the wide-screen TV with Huw and a couple of cans. And apart from sex and discussing work ideas, he and Maggie had little in common. She was a connoisseur and enjoyed the finer things in life like avant-garde art and opera. Owen preferred the *X-Files*, *The Simpsons* and Blur.

"Short and curlies, Owen," Huw said as he saw Owen rushing to get ready for another night of lust chez Maggie.

"What?" Owen snapped. He was tired and didn't fancy catching the bus to Penarth to see Maggie again.

"She's your boss and you can't say no, so she's got you by the short and curlies!" Huw laughed.

"It's not a joke." Owen turned to look at him morosely. "If I say I'm too busy, she sulks and is a bitch to me in work."

"What? I thought she, more than anyone, would be professional," Huw said in surprise.

"Why would you think that? Is shagging your twenty-five year old researcher professional?" Owen asked.

"You have to get out of this mate."

"Yes, and wave goodbye to my career at the same time."

"Not necessarily. There are other TV companies in Cardiff, aren't there?"

"Well, yeah, but I really want to do this sci-fi series."

"You've got a choice." Huw looked serious for once. "Your life, or your career."

Owen nodded and grabbed his jacket.

"You look like you're going to a funeral, not to have a

night of mind-blowing sex!" Huw laughed and he watched his friend walk out of the room like a zombie.

Huw's words echoed in Owen's head as the bus chugged its way to Penarth. He couldn't carry on like this. Why should he jump every time Maggie lifted her little finger? He was a man wasn't he? He'd have to finish things with her once and for all before he lost control of his life completely. Why, only last week, she'd hinted that she expected him to move in with her in a few months, then they could "come out" to everyone in the office! He knew some of his more savvy workmates were starting to doubt the close "working" relationship between Maggie and him and it was only a matter of time before the news broke. How would his mother feel if she knew he was seeing a woman only a few years younger than she was? Tonight, yes, he'd finish with her tonight...or maybe tomorrow.

The following day, after another memorable night in Maggie's bed, Owen had made his decision. Two weeks later, he'd managed to get a researcher job with another, smaller TV company, which was run by two middle-aged men, with no sexy cougars in sight so he could at last escape Maggie's clutches. He'd got Huw to write him a reference and his Media Studies Lecturer wrote him a glowing testimonial – Owen knew Maggie wasn't reference material, not under these rather unfortunate circumstances!

By the middle of the following week he'd surreptitiously packed all his work things away in a box and on the Thursday evening left Maggie an email notifying her of his resignation. He'd selected the day of his departure carefully. He knew Maggie would be out on location the following day. He didn't want any unfortunate scenes at work. He didn't say goodbye to any of his work colleagues on the Friday. The "battery farm" work ethic didn't really breed intimacy. He knew that he'd *never* ever have another relationship with a work colleague, it just wasn't worth it, it was a lesson learned – never shit on your own doorstep. It was lucky he'd got the other job and signed the contract; he wouldn't put it past Maggie to blackball him (she already had physically!). Owen had left the numerous gifts Maggie had bought him over the course of their relationship in her desk drawer. The gold cufflinks, the Paul Smith calfskin wallet, the expensive aftershave… He didn't want her to think that he'd only been in it for the gifts, the expensive dinners and the champagne. As he'd said in his email, he thought the world of her but he wasn't man enough for her yet. He hoped she'd understand.

Chapter 4

Mari

Mr Desperate, 2002

Mari was getting bored of playing Tetris on her mobile phone. Here she was, sitting like muggins, in a bar on her lonesome waiting for a bloke that she barely remembered for that awkward first date. And he was late. Real life wasn't like *This Life* and she had to remember that, instead of thinking she was TV's Anna the sexy solicitor everyone fancied. The only things she could remember about David were that he was tall, dark, quite cute – oh, and had excellent dancing and kissing skills. They'd shared a kiss in a bar last Saturday and had been texting and emailing flirty messages to each other all week. His features were cloudy in her mind because she had been pretty intoxicated when they'd met.

"Hello!"

Mari raised her head from her mobile phone but it wasn't David smiling at her but some other guy. He seemed familiar with his freckles and warm smile. Then she remembered! That bloody bloke who went for the researcher job at Reel-Time! Pretending to be nerdy and shy whereas he must be a complete barracuda given he got the job.

"Sorry, but do I know you?"

"We went for the same job in Reel-Time about a year ago?"

"Oh, yes." What did he want? A chance to brag? "You got the job I take it?"

"Yes," he said, his cheeks reddening. She felt a bit guilty for being a snooty bitch – he was very endearing, in an annoying sort of way.

"Don't worry, I got a job with Celt TV. How are things with Reel-Time?"

"I don't work there any more… It was like a battery farm… Not much room for creativity," the boy explained.

"Oh, and where are you now?" Mari enquired, hoping that David wouldn't turn up and see her chatting to another bloke. Actually, that might go in her favour and make her look popular and anyway she was enjoying chatting to him, he had an easy way about him.

"I'm working with Impetus now on a kids' series."

"Well, it's nice to see you again…"

"Owen."

"Owen. I'm Mari. See you around…"

"Are you going to see a film later?"

Mari was a tad puzzled with this line of enquiry until she realised that Rosie's Bar was literally next door to the Cinema Multiplex. "No, I don't think so, although I've heard good things about *Secretary*."

Secretary was a new cult film, which involved spanking and sado-masochism. Mari had mentioned it to test Owen to see if he knew his onions and to see him blush!

Bingo! He flushed and said, "Yes, I've heard it's quite hardcore – perhaps we could go together sometime to see it? As we keep bumping into each other like this!"

Mari laughed and was quite tempted but then she saw David approaching the table. "I'll get in touch if tonight doesn't work out!"

Owen smiled at her before going to sit nearby. Typical! You can't get a date in months and then two men come along at once!

"Mari!"

David stood at her side. Her face lit up as she realised he was good-looking after all. Fair play to her and her "radar" – even her beer goggles were 20/20 where attractive men were concerned! Unlike poor Helen, who had the unfortunate habit of pulling all the gargoyles in the city after too much cava... Mari noticed with relief that David was happy to see her too. She smiled at him. "Hiya David."

He gave her a quick peck on the lips. "Hi Mari. Great to see you again. Would you like a drink?"

"I've got one thanks."

"I'll just go to the bar and get a pint." Mari watched him walk to the bar and was impressed. He was tall, 6"2 at least, muscly and his bottom was very attractive in his trendy jeans. Now to turn on a bit of a charm offensive and who knew, perhaps she'd actually have a boyfriend before the evening was out.

David returned to the table carrying a pint of lager. "So how's work been for you this week?"

"OK, quite busy..."

"Yes, it must be so exciting working in TV..."

Exciting, my arse, Mari thought. Working for a Welsh TV Company wasn't what you'd call exciting. Mari had become quite embittered. The only thing that kept her going in her job was the enjoyment of working creatively, even though she spent most of her time developing stupid projects written by talentless writers for thoughtless commissioners with low budgets.

"It looks exciting, but it's not. It's like any other job really."

David leant forward in his chair, "I've always wanted to write scripts. How would I go about it?"

Mari's heart sank as she recognised the glint of the overly ambitious fanatic in David's eyes. *Fuck's sake!* He had no interest in her! He just wanted a job in TV!

David must have noticed her frown. He grabbed her hand, "Mari, are you OK?"

Mari looked at his handsome face and thought perhaps she might have been overly sensitive, perhaps the bloke was just showing interest in her work out of politeness. She smiled at him, "I'm OK, thanks, just some brain-freeze because of the ice in this drink… How was work with you this week? Kids behaving OK?"

David had told her in one of his many emails that he was undertaking a Teacher Training course. He laughed. "Oh, same old same old, you know. Stupid, cheeky kids and bitter, uncaring teachers. I don't want to teach as a career, I'm only doing the course to keep Mum and Dad happy. Something to keep me occupied until I win my first Oscar!"

Mari laughed. "Winning an Oscar is quite difficult you know."

David nodded and said brightly, "I know but I've written something that'll be a sure fire hit! It's about a talented disabled boy who falls in love with his sexy yet sensitive young nurse. A cross between *Forrest Gump* and *Billy Elliot.*"

Like you then! Mari thought to herself. *Winning an Oscar!* David was talking himself into the category of all-round wanker.

"My friends say it's really funny but touches the emotions, too. Perhaps you could show it to your boss sometime?"

The flattery didn't work. Mari could see the naked ambition in his eyes. It was obvious he only wanted one thing: an introduction to her boss, not a loving and romantic relationship.

"Listen, David," Mari said. "If you want career advice, you might as well arrange an appointment directly with my boss, OK? I thought you wanted to have a drink with me to get to know me better, not to get free career advice!"

"Sorry, Mari, I didn't mean anything like that. I haven't stopped thinking about you since…erm…last Saturday. You're so pretty and clever… Your emails were so funny and…interesting!"

He reached for her hand but Mari knew that there was no point in continuing with this charade. There was an awkward silence.

"Listen, I'll get you a drink from the bar so we can get to know each other properly. No more shop talk, I promise."

"G and T, please," Mari said faking a smile. *Good!* Whilst the twat was getting a drink from the bar, she could send a hurried text to Sara: "Get me out of here!" She looked over at Owen who was sitting with a very chatty, good looking girl – she felt a surprising sting of jealousy. He obviously wouldn't be interested in going to see the movie with Mari, now.

By the time David had returned from the bar, Mari had succeeded in sending her SOS.

"So, you fancy moving on somewhere else after this drink?"

Ugh! How had she ever thought he was good-looking? He was as slimy as a slug! Come on, Sara, she prayed to herself. *Come on!* And then, hallelujah, her mobile phone rang. "Oh, I wonder who that could be?"

"Let it ring."

"It's Sara, my best mate. I better answer. She wouldn't be ringing unless it was really important." Mari said. She answered the phone giving a performance that would have made Meryl Streep look like a member of the Neath Am-Dram society.

"Hi Sara, What's wrong? Have you phoned an ambulance? OK, don't worry, I'll be with you as soon as I can!"

She looked at David and feigned disappointment. "I'm really sorry, but there's a crisis at home, I have to go."

"What's wrong?" David asked, stroking her arm. *Balls!* She didn't think she'd need a full explanation, she'd hoped the word "ambulance" would have been enough for him, the nosy beggar!

"Erm…my friend, Helen's fallen down the stairs in the flat and Sara thinks she's broken her leg. The ambulance is on its way. I'll have to go home, Sara doesn't drive." Phew! That sounded relatively plausible, even though she didn't drive either and she was two gins over the limit. Anyway, she didn't care if he did doubt her excuse. After all, she didn't want to see the loser ever again.

"Oh, what a shame," David said. "And I was so looking forward to tonight. But I understand completely. I'll nip into Celt to see you for a cuppa sometime."

Jesus! It would be easier getting dog muck off your stilettos than saying goodbye to this idiot! "Erm, OK," Mari said. "But the boss doesn't like visitors calling without an appointment. I'll ring you so we can arrange something. Bye!"

"Come here!" David said, grabbing her arm as she tried to leave the table. "No kiss goodbye?"

"Sorry!" Mari said leaning over to give him a perfunctory kiss on the cheek. As she walked out, she turned back to look at David and saw that he was supping his pint and chatting happily on his mobile phone. Not that worried, then…

Mari sat in the taxi on her way to meet up with Sara and Helen in the Welsh Club in town, head down and dejected. Another excruciating date and a new twat to add to her already vast collection. She hoped she wouldn't see his smarmy smile ever again…

The following week Mari had deleted several emails and texts from David without bothering to respond to any of them. When would he get the message that she wasn't interested? If he sent one more message, she'd tell him the truth: that he was a smarmy bugger who just wanted to use her to get a job in TV. That would teach him a lesson! But she didn't hear anything for the next two days and hoped that he'd got the message, at long last.

Tuesday afternoon Mari was busy editing one of the dire scripts by her boss's latest protégée. She was furious – she was having to rewrite a script that had cost the company £5k and must have taken all of a week to write it was so bad! And she was only scraping by on £18k a year herself! It just wasn't fair. The phone rang. It was Nia, one of her co-producers and her best friend at work.

"Hi Mari. Listen, I wanted to warn you, that bloke you went on the date from hell with… Well, he's on the way to see you! Mandy let him through before I had a chance to stop her!" Mandy was the company receptionist – a lovely girl but not one of the brightest bulbs in the box.

Thank God Nia had been in reception to warn her about the incoming invasion.

Shit! She couldn't bear to see David again. She looked around vainly searching for an escape route. Thank God she was on the ground floor. There was only one way out… She opened her office window and jumped. She knocked on Carys's window. Carys was busy editing and jumped when she saw Mari's anxious face pressed against the glass.

"Mari, what the hell are you doing?" Carys asked as she helped Mari into her office.

"Hiding! D'you remember that creepy bloke I went on a date with last week? Well, Nia rang me to tell me he's on the way to see me. Lock the door, for God's sakc, in case he comes in here to look for me!"

Carys started to giggle like a school girl. The girls hid bchind the door listening carefully but they couldn't hear anything. After a few minutes, Carys said, "I'll go out and see if the coast's clear." She was obviously enjoying the subterfuge.

"No!" Mari grabbed her hand in a panic. "That's what he wants. He'll be sure to find me then!"

After a further five minutes of sweating and waiting, Mari rang reception. "Mandy, has he gone…? Who? That awful bloke you sent down to see me! He's using me to get a job here…! No, he isn't nice, Mandy. If he comes in again, tell him I'm away on leave or something!"

She returned to her desk, still jumpy, in case David leapt out at her from some corner. She noticed that he'd left a note and his script on her desk, too! She threw a contemptuous look at the title *Wheels of Love*. Ugh! Cheesy and derogatory to the disabled too! She threw the script unceremoniously into the bin.

It took three weeks, and several pairs of laddered tights, of Mari climbing in and out of her office window to avoid him before the visits ceased. In the end she had to send him a surly text, "Please don't come and see me at work again. My boss isn't interested in your script, so there's no other reason for you to come and harass me at work. Piss off."

"Don't you think that's a bit harsh?" Carys enquired.

"There's only way to deal with him, Carys. He's turning into a stalker, you know!" He didn't return her text and his visits stopped after that. But a few months later – she was waiting in the BBC's reception area before a meeting – she saw David walking head held high, like an emperor, towards her. Shit! She hoped he wasn't going to make a scene in front of everyone. She started to regret that she'd sent that mean message to him.

"Mari…" He looked down his nose at her.

"David," she said, with as much derision as possible in her voice.

"I was very disappointed to read your text," David said smoothly. "I wanted us to work together on my script. It would have been an excellent opportunity for you to climb the career ladder and become a good producer."

"Oh well, I'm sure I'll survive somehow," Mari said, picking up a magazine and starting to read it, hoping he'd get the hint and bugger off.

"Well, it doesn't matter anyway," David said. "I'm developing the script here with the BBC. A much better company with excellent producers who appreciate talent when they see it."

"Oh, which poor sucker did you manage to pull here then?"

"I don't know what you're talking about." David smiled one more time before turning on his heel and walking towards a glamorous middle-aged woman who clasped his arm territorially. Mari watched David smile his smarmy smile at her and kiss her on the lips. *Ugh!* She was old enough to be his mother… Suddenly, Mari recognised the woman. Maggie Lewis, the Reel-Time Drama boss and the biggest maneater in Welsh media! What a perfect couple!

Owen

Miss Web, 2002

Owen wasn't sure if he was doing the right thing taking Huw's advice. Finding love online was clinical to say the least and had a whiff of the "sad" about it. His hands paused on the computer keyboard as he pondered the wisdom of his actions.

"Oi – what's the next category?" Huw, sitting like a Lord on the sofa in his fluorescent underpants, was chomping crisps noisily.

"This is silly," Owen said looking over at his friend. "Who do you think really goes on these websites? Desperate and ugly people who can't scare up a date, that's who!"

"Yes, people like you, Owen, old son."

"Thanks a lot, Huw."

"I'm only joking man! You're so sensitive. Listen, they can't all be ugly and desperate. There must be someone like you out there – shy without enough confidence to make the first move in a crowded bar."

"I don't know, Huw. I feel weird about it…"

"Well, you don't *have* to go out with them – nobody's forcing you, you know. But if you see one that looks nice and sounds half sane, well, what's the harm in having an innocent little date? The girls aren't exactly queuing up at your door at the moment are they?"

Owen considered this for a second and opened his mouth to answer but didn't get a chance.

"Listen to your Uncle Huw, now. *Carpe diem*, he who dares… What if the woman of your dreams is on the website waiting for you and you lose the chance of meeting her 'cause you're too scared to take a chance? Wouldn't that be a tragedy?"

"Tragedy? It'll be a bigger bloody tragedy if I can't even get a date on this crappy website, after all, I really will have reached rock-bottom – Loserville!"

"Stop whining will you and get on with it! God…!" Huw puffed.

"I don't see you putting your name down," Owen said.

"I have a very satisfactory arrangement with Elin, thank you. I don't need "extras" at the moment," Huw said contentedly. Elin was on standby when Huw fancied sex at the end of a night out. They had a mutual no strings arrangement and they were both content with it, well, so far anyway.

Owen turned back to the website. "Sex," he said sounding glum.

"Yes, please!" Huw laughed.

"Oof! That joke's so old Huw... Right, male seeking female..." Owen added as he ticked the appropriate box.

"Well, yeah, if you don't want to try the other side, 'cause you're not having much luck with the fairer sex are you?" Huw laughed again.

"Listen Huw, if you don't want to help, just piss off. Now, 'What are you looking for?'"

"Sex!" Huw said again.

"Yes, but I need to put down a selection from companionship, music lover, easy going, attractive... before I'll get much chance at that, though, won't I?" Owen read some more options from the website. "Shared interests, own home, financially stable..."

"Hold on! Do you think you're going to find Miss Perfect on a website like this?" Huw spluttered – his Cheesy Wotsits flying all over the carpet.

"Well," Owen responded, trying to be positive for once. "As you said earlier, there has to be someone like me on this site... Normal enough but who hasn't met the right one yet..."

"Normal, I'd never call you normal, Owen!" Huw scoffed.

Owen ignored him. "Right, shut your cakehole and let me tick the boxes. How old –18–25?"

Huw scratched his head thoughtfully and said, "You know, I think you should go for someone a little more mature. You're 26 now mate!"

"OK then, 25–35?" Owen suggested.

Huw sat up full of excitement. "Yes, 35, the magic number! They're in their prime at 35!" But then he frowned and added, "But then again, she might have a couple of rug-rats by then and an ex-husband that looks like Vinnie Jones… You better say 21-30. A nice cut-off point there." He nodded sagely and resumed his crisp eating.

Owen ticked the final box puffing with relief. "OK, off it goes! And if you say anything to anyone about this, you're dead!"

"Take a chill-pill will you?" Huw guffawed, spitting half-chewed cheesy pulp into his lap. "Hey, I'm looking forward to seeing the specimens that will be answering you back!" He rubbed his hands with anticipation.

A week later, and although Owen was loath to admit this, and definitely wouldn't to Huw, the damn dating website was becoming an addiction. He kept going back to check his profile so he could keep tabs on the number of women who'd been checking him out. But as he'd suspected from day one, most of them were complete dodos. Too old, too fat, too ugly, too stupid, too boring, too weird and in one case, too married.

"Bloody Hell!" Huw roared as he read the responses over Owen's shoulder. "Look what this one says; 'You have the kindest eyes ever in your photo and very sexy arms...'"

Owen had chosen the only cool photo of himself to represent his profile, of him playing guitar at an old college gig.

Huw continued, "'I'd love to take that lucky guitar's place so we could make sweet music together...'"

"*Bleurgh!*" Owen said with disgust. "She's horrendous!"

"Well, she may not be the next Oscar Wilde, but at least the girl is keen!"

"Too cheesy!" Owen grumped. "And I bet she uses 'LOL' and 'OMG' in her text-speak too!"

"God! You're picky!" Huw scoffed. "Well, what about this one then, 'Star 75' – she sounds OK..."

"Apart from the deluded nom de plume, her profile sounds relatively normal."

"Yeah, and, that's what you wanted wasn't it? A nice, normal girl to have a simple uncomplicated date with and if possible, a bit of a work out for poor John Thomas, he's been a prisoner for far too long in that chastity belt of yours!"

Owen pondered the truth in Huw's words.

"OK, look carefully at her photo, she *is* pretty isn't she?"

Both men leaned forward and studied the girl's photo

carefully. She was curvy yet slim. Her dress was satisfactory, showing a potentially interesting cleavage but not too slutty. Her face was open, her skin clear, her eyes a dancing brown and her smile wide and unaffected. Yes, Owen thought to himself, he quite fancied her. But his heart wasn't turning somersaults… Was he expecting too much from a low-res photo? He hadn't even met her yet!

"She's very fit," Huw said. But then he added a note of caution, "Of course, one must consider whether it's a recent photo…"

"What do you mean?" Owen looked at him in alarm.

"Well, she might be cheating… After all you're only 23 in the photo you chose for the website…"

"Yeah, but what's three years? I haven't changed that much."

"It's a lot for some people. Take Elvis – in 1968 he was a 'lean, mean, fighting machine' on his comeback tour – remember that awesome leather jumpsuit…? But fast forward three years and after a smorgasbord of pancakes and burgers he was like a mammoth in a mumu!"

"What the hell's a mumu?" Owen asked.

"Giant Hawaiian frocks for the larger sized gentleman or lady. You might recall Homer Simpson had to resort to a mumu in that episode when he had an eating disorder…"

"Right, I don't want to hear anymore! I'm going to ask Star75 out for a drink next week!"

"OK, you know best. But just watch out that she isn't really Star55!" Huw warned.

Owen sat by the window of Rosie's Bar, Cardiff Bay, with his heart in his throat. He kept watching the girls who were walking into the bar and praying when he saw a particularly unattractive specimen that it wasn't Star 75. He hoped she'd recognise him from his photo and that he really hadn't changed too much. Shit! What if she thought he was a munter and legged it?

He'd been pleased to spot Mari, the pretty girl from Reel-time there. It was a shame he hadn't seized his chance and asked for her phone number. He cursed his infernal shyness. But then again, he knew she'd turn him down, she was obviously waiting for her date to arrive. Even though, when the guy turned up he was a slimy twat in a suit. Anyway, he had to keep focused. He was here to meet with Star75 – if she turned up… Then he saw her and, thank God, she was even prettier than her photo. *Shit!* Would she fancy him or was she out of his league? But then she walked towards him with a broad smile on her pretty face.

"Agent76?" she whispered hopefully. Yes, Agent76 had seemed a good idea when he and Huw had been re-watching their XFiles dvds but now it just seemed stupid.

"Erm… yeah," Owen said. "Please, sit down," he gestured vaguely at the chair next to his.

The girl sat down and pulled out a pack of cigarettes from her handbag, offering him one. Thank God, she was a smoker! He'd been dying for a fag but hadn't dared in case she was an anti-smoking zealot.

"Maria," she told him with a coquettish smile.

"Owen," he smiled back at her. "Would you like a drink, Maria?"

"White wine, please."

"Cool," Owen said, stumbling awkwardly as he noticed her rather sumptuous breasts under her lacy top when he stood up to go to the bar. God was generous... sometimes...

An hour later and Owen had changed his mind completely about the generosity of the "man upstairs". Getting a conversation going with this woman was quite a challenge. As Frasier, his favourite sitcom character, said, this wasn't "small talk" this was "teeny talk"! What a shame; she was such a sexy and attractive girl, too, with long mahogany hair cascading in waves around her shoulders. He quite liked the sparkling brown eyes and long eyelashes too. He tried again, "So you're from Penarth then, Maria?"

Maria answered with an affected twang, "Yes, Penarth. Mum and Dad wanted a little pied-a-terre by the sea... Of course, we're London Welsh originally."

Owen faked an interest in her lineage. "Oh, I see, so did you go to that famous Welsh school in London then?"

Maria laughed, a sound that reminded Owen of cats fighting in his backyard during mating season, "No, I went to Howell's Girls School in Cardiff, but Mum always says that we're really from London."

Kill me now! Owen thought to himself. Bloody Huw and his stupid ideas.

"Oh, I see." Owen racked his brains for something else to say. "So what do you do then, Maria?"

"Well, I'm on work experience at the moment with the Welsh Tourist Board, although there aren't many tourist attractions in Cardiff, unfortunately!"

Owen's hackles shot up, he thought Cardiff was the best city in the world, but he held his tongue and asked politely, even though he had no interest whatsoever in the boring sow. "So what do you want to do afterwards?"

Maria laughed her grotesque laugh and placed her hand flirtatiously on his arm, "Take it easy, we haven't finished our first drink yet!"

Oh God, what a crap joke! Owen faked a smile. "No, I meant your job…"

Maria tutted under her breath, "Yes, I know… Lighten up, Owen! I feel as if I'm in a job interview here!"

There was an awkward pause and Owen imagined tumbleweed blowing across Rosie's Bar. What should he say now? Was there any point pursuing this further? Wouldn't be better to say bye-bye to the dumb bint and not waste any more time?

Maria mistook his silence for nerves, "Oh, poor Owen. Is this your first date from the website?"

Owen stared at her before answering, "Erm…yes. What about you?"

Maria giggled. "Oh good God, no! I'm an old hand by now. 'Try before you buy,' that's my motto!"

Owen's heart fell into his trainers. As usual, he'd selected the last turkey in the shop. Almost to himself he said, "I don't think I fancy a late night tonight…"

But luckily Maria was still talking and hadn't heard a word he was saying,

"Yes, it can be tricky to get the chemistry right with these things. But I feel really positive about you and I, Owen, I think we've got something interesting here…"

"Do you?" Owen was shocked, her other dates must have been truly awful. Then he noticed out of the corner of his eye that Mari, the girl from Reel-time, was leaving the bar with her date! Shit! It's a pity he couldn't go after her and ask for her number. But no he was stuck here with Scary Spice and there was no escape. He turned his attentions back to Maria who was smiling. To his great surprise she started playing footsie with him beneath the table. Owen started to reconsider… Well, she was pretty and he hadn't had sex for ages… Perhaps the relationship would grow after they slept together… Then a little voice piped up inside his head, that little angelic voice which would always prick his conscience if he was planning something dodgy, in particular if he started thinking with his penis and not his brain. A relationship was supposed to grow *before* you slept with a girl!

This was all Huw's fault. OK, he wasn't going to sleep with her. Not at all, never, no way! Well, perhaps not…

Shit! Where had his socks got to? Owen crept around Maria's room like a thief, picking up his clothes quietly from the floor and getting dressed. Maria snored gently in bed and Owen prayed she wouldn't wake up and catch him fleeing the scene of the crime. Why the hell had he slept with her last night? Yes, OK, the sex was all right because she had a really sexy body; massive boobs, a tiny waist and surprisingly long and supple legs… He smiled as he remembered their sexual gymnastics but he also remembered that Maria insisted on talking whilst they were at it. He stumbled over his jeans as he struggled to get dressed and held his breath for a few seconds lest she wake up and discover his cowardice. The internal monologue inside his head gave him comfort and calmed his nerves somewhat. All he had to do was put on his trainers and leave… Then in an hour or two send her a nice polite text telling her, "Thanks, but no thanks." Yes, the coward's way but the easiest way to get out of a pickle like this one…

Maria stirred suddenly and sighed softly. Owen froze like a statue, his heart beating deafeningly loud. But after a few seconds, she started to snore once more and Owen resumed his escape. If he could get out unscathed from this bedroom, he promised God and all his cherubs that he would never ever date a girl from the internet again! Although the sex had been quite acceptable, things had taken a severe turn for the worse as Maria seemed to think it was sexy to chatter throughout the act itself. She spoke about every topic under the sun, including her father's Shetland ponies, and with Owen doing his best moves on her!

This was the last time Owen Davies would take Huw's advice on romance. From now on, he would depend on the old fashioned way of meeting girls – getting pissed on a night out and hoping for the best.

Chapter 5

Mari

Mr Nice, 2003

Mari didn't know why she'd agreed to come to the "Single and Mingle" night at the Wharf Pub in the Bay. It was totally desperate. But Sara had persuaded her by saying, "Who knows, perhaps the perfect man will be there tonight and if you don't go, then you'll miss your chance and he'll end up with someone else… Wouldn't that be an utter tragedy, your perfect man with another woman?"

"Not really," Mari answered. "Because I wouldn't know that he exists, so I wouldn't know what I've lost."

"Well, you know now 'cause I've just told you!" Sara said victoriously, dragging her up from the sofa. "Mari, you're 27 not 87! And you need to enjoy life. You haven't had a date since…" Sara paused, as they knew she was about to name "he who must not be named".

"Mike," Mari finished the sentence for her. Mike had been another disaster – a real mummy's boy, who sadly had invited his mum to their first date and as a double

123

whammy had confessed to her in an apologetic email a few days later that he was gay.

"OK, but I know the reason why you want me to go with you; you want to chat up that sexy barman we saw last time!"

"Well, that might also be true," Sara said, "but I really want you, my best friend, to enjoy a night out and a bit of fun, with no complications."

"There are always complications," Mari had said, bitterly, drawing the conversation to a close.

Anyway, here they were, standing self-consciously at the bar accompanied by Donna Summer's "I Feel Love" and surrounded by the city's desperados. "I've seen more talent in a morgue," Mari said.

"Well, we don't have to pull, you know, we can just mingle." Sara waved flirtily at the sexy barman who smiled back at her.

"Mingle? Mingle with whom? The Hannibal Lecter look-alike over there?" Mari said sharply, looking at a sorry specimen in front of her.

"Now, Mari, we agreed you were too choosy," Sara said patiently.

"When? When you tried to get me to go out with your cousin who looks like Bin Laden?"

"Hannibal Lecter, Bin Laden… You're obsessed!" Sara puffed into her cocktail.

"Well, most people know their murderers. That's a fact!"

"If I wanted to know that, I'd watch *Crimewatch*…"

"Yeah, even that would be better than watching Slimewatch – look at all these creeps!"

Donna Summer finally reached the extended version's climax and Mari noticed a tall skinny bloke in his early 30s dancing awkwardly beside them. He was quite good-looking in a nerdy way, even though he had a ginger-brown goatee.

Sara had clocked him too. "Oi, Mari, look, there's one there! And this one looks nice!"

"Gay, probably," Mari mumbled.

"Shh!" Sara said in a stage whisper. "He's coming over!"

It became quickly apparent that the man was primarily interested in Mari. He walked over to her and smiled shyly. Mari smiled back politely. God! She hoped he wouldn't use a cheesy chat up line on her. She steeled herself, ready for the worst.

"Hi. Are you a writer?"

"What?' Mari asked, was the guy psychic or something?

"You look like a writer," he said again, his kind eyes smiling at her. "Are you?"

Mari, to her great surprise, quite liked this unusual approach. "Well, I've written a few short stories," she said bashfully.

"Yes, and one was published in the *Western Mail*!" Sara said helpfully.

"I'd like to read these stories," the nerdy guy said.

Mari assessed him again and decided that she quite liked his nerdy appeal. After all – she'd tried plenty of conventionally good-looking types – tall, dark and handsome. How about trying a nerd? After all, he was quite cute in an Agent Mulder kind of way. She started to flirt with him gently, "Well, let's see shall we? It depends if you shave that little goatee off!"

He stroked his goatee thoughtfully and laughed.

"What's your name then?' Sara asked cheekily.

"Gary."

"Gary, meet Mari." They all laughed at the rhyme. Sara by now had had enough of the slow flirting and was keen to speed up the process. "Right then, Gary, you can come with me and get the drinks in."

For the next two years, Mari was absolutely convinced that Gary was indeed her Mr Perfect. He'd shaved off the goatee by their first date, a visit to the cinema to see *Donnie Darko*, the story of an awkward nerd that lived in fantasyland. And their names even rhymed! Sara got so far as suggesting that if they had a baby, they could call him Barry – just for a laugh! Everything Mari did was amazing in Gary's eyes. She was "gorgeous", even when she put two stones on and her dad said that she looked like Elvis in his Vegas years. But their romance was good. Like a boat on a millpond, chugging along happily, with no cloud on the horizon. And it was a no-brainer saying "Yes," when Gary went down on one knee in the Wharf, where they'd first met, on New Year's Eve and asked her to marry him. He was so nervous, his stutter was worse than usual. But his proposal was heartfelt. He had selected a very tasteful emerald ring from an antique shop in one of Cardiff's bijou arcades and Mari wore it proudly. At last, she had a steady and normal boyfriend. OK, he was a bit of a lapdog – waiting for her to take the lead in bed and agreeing with her every word, but he was safe and steady and she was almost thirty now and it was about time she settled down. She didn't want to be like those old biddies she saw on St Mary's St on Saturday nights – all peroxide, varicose veins and sequins, trying to pull the young yobs for a shag.

She'd survived Mr Awful Voice, Mr Desperate, Mr Dirty... What was wrong with settling for Mr Nice? She had to remember that Mr Perfect (a combo of Billy Crystal's humour in *When Harry Met Sally*; Johnny Depp's face in *Blow* and De Niro's air of danger in *Taxi Driver*) didn't exist, not really, apart from in her imagination.

They'd agreed on a summer wedding and selected Gary's birthday, August 20 as the prefect date. Mari's parents loved Gary. He had a secure job as a sound technician and his courteous and old-fashioned manners had betwitched her mum from the start. Then one day in June, two months before the big day, as they were working on the invitation list, her mum said something quite shocking.

"Mari, you do realise that Gary loves you more than you love him, don't you?" She looked Mari straight in the eye as she sealed another wedding invitation.

"What?" Mari was shocked. Had she heard correctly? Or had Mum read her innermost thoughts somehow?

"Well, it's obvious the boy adores you. And although you're really fond of him, I don't think you feel the same way, not really…"

Typical! She always ruined everything. "Mum! I think the world of Gary! Why would you say such a thing?"

"OK, I may be wrong, but please make sure you're marrying Gary for the right reasons… It's hard enough to make a marriage work as it is—"

"I *am* sure, thanks, Mum. Now, don't say anymore will you? You'll ruin everything!"

After that Mari's mum threw herself into the wedding arrangements with the discipline of a hard-core marine and not another doubt was voiced. She was in her element haggling with the cake woman, the florist, and the venue staff. All the arrangements were completed by July. But the seed had been sown and as the wedding day got nearer and nearer, Mari's doubts started to niggle away at her, especially after she had a terrible row with Gary's mum, Glenda.

Glenda was the complete opposite of Mari's mum – very bohemian – and she lived in an old stone house in Machynlleth, full to the brim with cats. Mari, who'd experienced a very antiseptic upbringing with her fastidious mum, had quite a shock when she saw Glenda placing empty lasagne bowls on the floor so the cats could have the scraps. Yes, Glenda was quite different to the conventional Welsh "Mam". She was a very well respected historian in academic circles, smoked like a steam engine and had decided on a single life after divorcing Gary's dad (a rather feckless arty type who loved the whisky bottle more than he did his wife) in the 1970s. Gary and his sister, Lisa, were her everything and although she wasn't contributing a penny to the wedding (Mari's dad was footing the bill), she did have some very strong ideas about the arrangements. She'd been phoning Gary for months asking him to add her fifth cousins (who lived in the South of England somewhere and were complete strangers to Gary) to the invitation list. Gary, in his peace-loving way had tried to explain to his mum that the additional £200 to feed this bunch of strangers was too much to ask, especially as they'd never met. But she wouldn't give in. If the cousins weren't invited, then neither she nor Lisa would attend the wedding. As they were his only family, this threatened to destroy the whole day.

Mari felt the blood rushing to her ears when she

watched Gary turn into a pale waxwork as he listened to his mum yelling down the phone. *Right!* She'd tolerated the mad old bitch's behaviour for months. If Gary wasn't man enough to sort this out, then she would have to do it for him. Mari grabbed the phone and said in her fake nice voice, "Hi Glenda, Mari here. Now, what's the problem?"

"Well, Mari,' Glenda answered all hoity-toity. "I think it's an absolute disgrace! You're treating our family like blacks! In my day you'd invite both halves of the family!"

"Well, Glenda, why don't you *pay* half then?" And with that, Mari slammed the phone down. That would teach her, the madam!

After quite a discussion with her mum and dad, Mari had to agree to the old witch's blackmail and the unknown fifth cousins were invited to the wedding, for Gary's sake. But as she told him, she wouldn't speak to Glenda on the day, and the bitch wouldn't be in the family wedding photos either. Gary accepted this quietly, without quarrel or protest.

As she watched him speak quietly to his mum on the phone, explaining the new arrangements, Mari realised that she didn't respect him at all. He should have sorted this himself. Glenda was his mum. Why was he so happy to leave it all to her? Why didn't he say to Mari that he wanted his mum and his family to be in the wedding photos? That's what Mari wanted him to say. Why couldn't he show some backbone for once? Did she really want to spend the rest of her life with such a limp lettuce of a man? But it was too late. The wedding arrangements were moving ahead like a relentless juggernaut and Mari knew her family would be hugely disappointed and ashamed if she cancelled the big day now. She had to go on with the show, anything would be better than destroying Gary and her parents' big day.

Gary hadn't noticed anything was wrong; he was as loving and tender as ever. But Mari just didn't feel the same towards him. Every time he wanted to make love, she'd find some lame excuse to get out of it. Her period had arrived or she had a headache (the old classic) or she was tired/stressed/distracted with the wedding. She decided, after poor Gary had tried, after one drunken night out, to undo her bra-clasp, that she needed a better excuse.

"Look, Gary, I think it would be far more romantic if we didn't have sex until we're married, now. I'm quite old fashioned about things like that and I think our honeymoon should be really special…"

Poor Gary went along with her wishes (as usual) and gave her kudos for the romantic gesture. *Thank God!* She wouldn't have to fake an orgasm for at least a month.

A fortnight before the wedding Gary and Mari went to the small arty cinema in Chapter Arts Centre to see her favourite film, *Run Lola Run*; a German film in which the girl views three different endings to her story.

Gary had gone to the loo so Mari had bagged a place in the queue in the foyer for their tickets. And who happened to be standing in the queue, looking rather lonely but Owen, the guy from Reel-Time – as Mari had started to call him in her head. After her pathetic date with David, she had toyed with sending him a friendly email, to ask him out on a date to see *Secretary* but she hadn't bothered as he seemed quite engrossed in his date that evening.

Anyway, he was looking really cute tonight in his Super Furry Animals T-shirt, jeans and Converse. And was it her imagination but was he cuter than she remembered? Shit! Why did she have to be here with Gary…

"Mari! How are you?"

Mari turned around and smiled at Owen, "Owen, hi! Nice to see you. Here to see *Run Lola Run*?"

"Yup, but couldn't rustle up a date. Do you fancy watching it with me?"

Damn, she would have loved to have watched the movie with Owen but no, Gary was back and had put a territorial arm around her shoulders.

"Gary, this is my work friend, Owen. Owen, this is Gary…"

"Nice to meet you," Owen smiled.

"Owen's on his lonesome tonight, Gary, so I said it would be OK for him to join us…"

She didn't really know why she invited Owen, but she didn't want an awkward romantic evening with Gary, not with her ambivalent feelings about him at present. Owen would be a welcome distraction.

Of course, Gary was so polite and easygoing he didn't object to this unexpected ménage à trois and it gave Mari an opportunity to perv over cute and charismatic Owen, who was looking super attractive this evening. Why hadn't she noticed that before?

"I don't want to intrude." Owen hesitated.

"No intrusion, my fiancée here is the nicest woman in Wales!" Gary beamed proudly. Mari winced slightly and tried to return his smile.

Did she imagine it or did Owen's face drop when he heard the word fiancée? Nah, it was wishful thinking, he'd never really made a move on her. And after all, she was with Gary – wasn't she?

As she ate her popcorn in the dark, Mari started to think more clearly about her situation, which had parallels to Lola's story. Might she be missing a "better ending" if she stayed with Gary? Was there another man out there that could give her everything; her truly perfect man? She looked surreptitiously at Gary as he gnawed his M&M's thoughtfully and then took a sneaky peek at Owen, who happened to look at her at the same time. They both smiled and Mari was almost convinced there was some chemistry between them. She decided to extend the evening to avoid yet another awkward bedroom scene with Gary after the film.

"Shall we go to the bar for a few drinks so we can dissect the film?" Mari asked Owen and Gary cheerily as they walked out of the cinema.

"Sounds good,' Owen said, 'I need a few beers after that – it was a bit of a headfuck wasn't it? But in a good way!"

"It was brilliant," Mari enthused. "I think Franka Potente is an amazing actress."

"Yes, definitely her best work," Owen agreed. "I don't think I've seen her in anything since the Bourne film."

"She was a bit wasted in that to be honest," Mari said.

Gary coughed and apologised, "Sorry guys, I don't really feel up to a pint tonight, I've got an early start tomorrow, remember Mari?"

Oh for fuck's sake! He was really cramping her style now. Mari toyed with the idea of telling Gary that she'd see him at home later and go for a drink with Owen anyway, but that would be a bad move at this point. She couldn't trust herself to behave with Owen, not with this inner turmoil going on in her head.

"No worries, some other time then," Owen said. "Nice to meet you Gary and nice to see you again Mari. Good luck with the wedding!"

Mari nodded, an involuntary shudder going through her as she heard the dreaded W word. She felt trapped and she wanted to escape. Just like Lola she might have an opportunity to change her own destiny and she knew she had to do it before the gold band was on her finger.

A week passed and Mari couldn't stop thinking about it. She knew she had to finish with Gary. And it wasn't because of Owen – she didn't even know the guy – not really! He was just a symptom – her lusting over him showed that she shouldn't really be with Gary – disappointed and out-of-pocket parents or not. She'd cooked Gary his favourite supper (well, this would be his *last* supper with her), of sausages and mash and gravy and he was happy swigging his San Miguel in the living room.

Mari joined him on the sofa nervously. She took a deep breath. There was only a week to go until the wedding. She had to find the balls to do this!

"Gary, I need to talk to you…"

"Mmm?" Gary said absently, his eyes glued to the TV.

"I…I don't think I can marry you…"

"What? Why?" He stared at her with his big Labrador brown eyes.

"I've been thinking a lot about us recently… And well, I don't think we really suit each other enough to get married…"

She noticed the tears beginning to gather at the corners of his eyes as he started to plead. She felt horrible.

"But two years, Mari… We've been together for two years… We've booked Cardiff Castle and everything…"

Mari grabbed his hand, "I know, but we'll get half our deposit back. I can't marry you, Gary. I can't – I don't… love you…"

"What? You said so many times…you did…"

Mari felt the tears running down her cheeks now. This was much harder than when she'd played the scene in her mind. She'd imagined Gary agreeing with her politely and hugging her thankfully for making the decision for them both before packing his bags very quickly. Gary wasn't going to give up easily.

"And so I do, but as a friend, that's all. Please, don't make things more difficult. I'm so sorry." She stared at him, hoping that he'd understand.

Gary stood up. "I can change… I can be more macho! Do you want me to be more macho?" Gary grabbed the bottle of San Miguel that he'd placed on the coffee table and threw it to the floor. It bounced on the carpet and rolled unharmed towards the fireplace.

Mari smiled at him. "You can't change who you are and you don't need to. You *are* a lovely man… And you'll find someone better, who'll suit you, I'm sure."

"Why have you changed your mind? I thought we were happy together?"

"We were," Mari consoled him. "You're great but I was staying with you because I was afraid of being single again. I was settling… And that's not fair on you or me."

"What? You're saying I'm not good enough for you or something?" There was just the hint of real anger in his eyes, now.

"No, not at all. To be honest, I think you're *too* good for me," Mari said, quickly. "I need someone who can give me a good bollocking, put me in my place a bit."

Gary pulled her towards him and squeezed her tight to his chest. "I'll do that, I promise. I love you so much… Can we please try again?" he pleaded. "You'll live to regret it if you don't."

But Mari knew in her heart that she couldn't try again. She pulled herself away from his arms. "I know I'm doing the right thing Gary. I don't love you enough to marry you and in time, you'll thank me, you'll see."

"Never, never!" Gary said, crying his heart out.

Mari fled the room, grabbed her case from the bedroom (she'd arranged to stay with Sara for a bit, just as backup) and made for the front door. As she reached for the lock, Gary turned to her and asked, "Is there anyone else?"

"No," Mari smiled, sadly. She couldn't tell him what she really felt, that there was no-one real, only a dream… But she knew, if she didn't leave now, then she'd always regret it and wonder what would have happened if she'd had the guts. As Sara said, it would have been easier to live a lie, to settle for a platonic marriage with Gary. It was a lot more scary to start from scratch once more and chase something or someone who could be pure fantasy.

"Look after yourself," she said.

"And you," Gary gave her a watery smile.

"I'll cancel the wedding…"

Mari was worried about what her mum and dad would say. Her dad wouldn't be impressed as he would lose his deposit. But she knew they'd support her. After all, her mum had been right when she'd said "Marriage is hard enough as it is." Leaving her and Gary's joint home for the last time that night, Mari turned her car towards the Bay and Sara's flat, and felt a mixture of relief and fear. She was alone again.

Owen

Miss Reunion, 2005

Owen had been delighted to bump into Mari again in the cinema – shame she was with that nerdy Gary guy. Had he imagined those sparks? Yes, he must have imagined it as she and Gary were getting married soon. No, she'd have to be filed under "the one that got away."

But of course, there was another one that *had* got away in his life. A major one.

There's one of these in everyone's past love lives. And

of course, the defining character in Owen's past was Michelle Richards... The mythical girl from *Baywatch*, the untouchable beauty with the silky blonde hair and luscious curves... The girl he'd vomited over... He promised himself their paths would cross again one day, when he'd be good enough to win her. And now it looked like the big day might have arrived, 14 years on from that first date (well, the only date). A high school reunion.

Owen had been on tenterhooks all day preparing for the big night and was determined that Michelle would see him as the attractive, eligible bachelor he now was and not the unfortunate spotty fool she'd encountered on their date. He was now a man, had gone through life's trials and emerged mature, like a fine wine... He wore his new shirt and Diesel jeans, had his barnet trimmed at Vidal Sassoon's; he looked completely different to his school self. No zits, no spiky haircut and no sex-related regurgitation issues. He hoped to God Michelle would actually be in attendance to see this amazing transformation. With luck she wouldn't have metamorphosed into a tragic middle-aged version of herself, either.

Owen and Huw stood by the bar watching the entrance to the pub carefully. But Huw had had enough after 15 minutes and was starting to whine. "Why did you persuade me to come to this crappy school reunion thing? If I'd wanted to keep in touch with those fuckers after leaving school, I would have, and I didn't."

Owen tried to raise his spirits. 'Apart from me, of course.' Huw laughed, always ready to pull his friend's leg.

"Yeah, well, you're a special case…with an emphasis on the 'special'."

"Yeah, right, *I* wasn't in the bottom set in maths."

"Everyone who's cool can't do maths. Anyway, I know why you've dragged me here tonight… *Michelle, ma belle…*" Huw started to sing the Beatles classic full throttle.

"Ssh!" Owen rebuked him, worried that someone might hear him. "Yeah, well, I need closure."

"Closure.' Huw scoffed. "What? Being sick over her wasn't enough? You want to finish the job this time?"

Typical! Huw had to remind him about that! "We said we wouldn't mention that ever again."

Huw smiled then stiffened in excitement like a meerkat. "OK, OK. Hey! Look, she's over there – OMG!"

Owen felt the panic flood through his body. What if she was ugly, fat or even worse, more beautiful than ever?

"I can't look!" Owen whispered in a panic. "Still fit?"

Huw was open mouthed. "Still…"

But Owen could see for himself as Michelle strode towards them in a skintight red Lycra dress that showed off her show-stopping body to perfection. No, she hadn't changed at all. If anything, she was prettier than ever, even though he didn't care for her hairstyle, which looked like a curly pineapple on top of her head or the abundance of fake tan and make-up on her face.

Michelle smiled confidently and turned to Owen, "Hi Owen, I thought it was you."

Owen smiled, still trying to keep his cool. "Hiya Michelle… You look… great."

Michelle laughed, "And you haven't changed at all, Owen!"

What the fuck! Hadn't changed at all? Was she blind or what? He could sense Huw smirking at his side and he said quickly, "Listen, do you want a drink Michelle? Huw was just on his way to the bar…"

Huw huffed reluctantly but understood that Owen wanted him to disappear. "Eh? Oh yeah, what's your poison Michelle? Thunderbird is it?" He laughed at his joke. Michelle said coolly, 'No, I don't drink Thunderbird these days. A large G and T please."

"Okey-dokey,"

Huw left for the bar. There was an awkward silence as Owen and Michelle stood with the multi-coloured disco lights spinning around them. He'd have to apologise to her about the vomiting issue, quick before Huw came back. "Listen, Michelle, I'm really sorry about what happened, you know, on that date."

"Yeah, well, I went off blow-jobs for a while after that, you know!"

"Yes, well, it had quite an effect on me as well."

"Water under the bridge and all that,' Michelle said lightly before changing the subject. "What are you doing with your life these days then? Married? Two-point-four kids or what?"

She must be fishing to see if he was single. He felt a bit more positive at this show of interest. "No, free and single you know… I'm a researcher for a TV company."

Michelle was obviously impressed, "Ooh…very glam!"

"Well, I don't know—"

"What are you working on?" Michelle asked excitedly. "*Dr Who*…? Or what's the other one?"

"*Torchwood*." Owen offered helpfully.

Michelle got very excited and shouted, "Oh my God, you're working on *Torchwood*?"

Owen's heart sunk to his shoes. "No, erm, *Farming Wales*."

"Oh… mmm. Good."

Shit! He was losing her. Why couldn't he lie and say he *was* working on *Torchwood*? He'd have to change the subject and try and get her attention back before it was too late… Right, how could he pull her back in? "Erm… I always thought you'd be a model… Are you?"

Michelle laughed proudly pushing her boobs out on auto-pilot. "Well, I did a bit of glamour work. But no, the kids keep me too busy these days."

Kids? Bollocks. Of course she'd have kids. How could

he expect a girl like this still to be on the shelf? What a fool! Owen tried to hide his disappointment and nodded nonchalantly whilst praying for Huw to come back from the bar with those drinks. The twat! This was all *his* fault, well almost all his fault.

Michelle continued to speak without noticing Owen's disappointed face. "Yes, well, they're with the ex- tonight."

The ex-? Might there be hope after all? He'd always fancied being one of those cool dads, the ones in the TV ads, playing footie with their cute sons in the garden, with the wife who looked like a supermodel calling them lovingly to the dinner table for some lovely Waitrose grub. Before he completely disappeared into his fantasy, he decided to come to the point. "The ex-? So you're single too?"

Michelle sighed as she heard the word ex- and lit a cigarette skilfully before replying, "Yes, it's a long story. But I'm happy now with my new partner…" She paused as she blew a perfect smoke ring around her head, "Rebecca."

Owen almost blew out the cigarette from his mouth as he heard the name.

"Rebecca?" he said, shocked.

Michelle laughed. "Yes. Once you've had muff, cock's never enough!" There was a pause after this as Owen wondered what he should say next and decided a sharp exit would be the best strategy.

Turning into a Welsh Hugh Grant, he said, "Muff... well...erm...very good. Well, I'd better go the bar and see where Huw is with those drinks." He smiled politely before jogging over to the bar and yelling, "Huw!" *Once you've had muff*, indeed! Another wasted evening.

Huw walked towards him with the drinks. He looked around for Michelle, "That was quick. Did you vomit over her again?"

Owen looked sombrely at his friend. "Michelle has emigrated to Lesbos."

They drank their pints considering this latest bombshell. "Oh, well," said Huw putting his hand on his friend's shoulder, "it's closure...of a kind."

Chapter 6

Mari

Mr Manic, 2006

"What's wrong?" Mari tried vainly to find a joke to lighten the awkward atmosphere between them.

"Mari. I've been thinking a lot about us and I think it's best that we finish…"

"What?" Mari couldn't believe her ears. "Why? You don't mean this. It's because of your depression."

"No, it's nothing to do with depression, at least not the way you mean. I think Sara and Helen are right. You're more like my mum than my girlfriend. And it's not fair that I'm putting such pressure on you…"

"I know I've been fussing a lot recently, Tim. But I'll try not to… But it's not a reason for us to finish things. You're getting better, the psychologist said so. Don't listen to Helen and Sara, they don't know jack!" Mari cursed her friends for talking about Tim in the hospital. It was obvious that he'd heard every word.

"Mari, at the moment I'm stable, but God knows how

I'll be tomorrow, next week or the week after… I'm just not in a good place to offer you what you need. A normal boyfriend that wants to go out and have fun and give you a great sex life… Not someone who keeps you on 'suicide watch' all the time!"

"Don't say that," Mari shouted, the tears running down her cheeks.

"You've been through such a lot because of me," Tim held her hand and tried his best to console her. "You know it's the best thing for both of us. You'll find someone else that suits you. Someone who isn't nuts!"

He laughed, but it wasn't a happy sound. The bitterness in it broke Mari's heart. "I don't want anyone else! I love you and I don't care about your illness!" Mari pleaded.

"You say that now, but in time, you'll be bitter and twisted and you'll start to hate me… And I don't want that. It's better to finish now while we can still be friends…"

"Friends! You know we can never be friends. I'm not friends with any of my ex-es!"

"In time perhaps?" Tim asked, full of hope.

Mari got up slowly. Her heart was in pieces but she could see from his eyes that he wasn't going to change his mind.

"Well…bye then! Thanks a lot for wasting my time." Her voice was brittle and hard, in contrast to the tears that were running down her cheeks. "I'm sorry, Mari."

There were no words left. She gave him one final look and ran out of the flat, slamming the front door behind her. She jumped into her car and started to drive like a bat out of hell. And she didn't see the man on the bike until she heard the thud on the side of her car.

9 months earlier

Mari woke up from a deep sleep with a start. She felt very odd. Where is she? She looked around and saw that she was in a very untidy bedroom. Some old battered posters hung on the wall – the Stone Roses, Nirvana and Blur. Blast from the past or what! A solitary cupboard stood in the far corner of the room, where a suit, shirt and tie was hanging askew. A vast mound of CDs was scattered on the floor beneath a huge stereo. There was an old cheap desk by the window that had a portable TV on it. A solitary goldfish swam in a plastic tank, which was perched precariously on the window sill. And an acoustic guitar sat in the only armchair.

Shit! She couldn't remember anything from the previous evening. She turned slowly to have a look at the creature that shared the bed with her. Phew! A very handsome boy slept by her side in a deep sleep. He had light brown hair, high cheekbones, gorgeous long eyelashes and full lips.

The previous night's events came back to her slowly.

Yes, she and Sara and Helen had gone out to Bar Cuba in town to celebrate Helen's birthday. They'd devoured a whole swimming pool's worth of Tequila between them and then… A Technicolor flash landed in her brain – she and the sleeping boy were snogging wildly at the bar… Now what was his name? And had she done more than slept with him? She doubted very much she had been in any state to do anything remotely sexual last night. She felt for her underwear nervously beneath the duvet and thanked baby Jesus that her trousers and knickers were still safely on her body.

The boy woke up slowly and she noticed he had the most stunning blue eyes she'd ever seen. Just like Steve McQueen in *The Thomas Crown Affair*. Shit! She hoped he wouldn't regret seeing her by his side! He might be out of her league!

He smiled at her with his eyes bearing into hers. "Come here," he said, wrapping his arms around her. Tim! Yes, Tim. Phew! Thank God she'd remembered his name. She moved towards him and snuggled up happily.

"How do you feel?" he asked stroking her hair.

"A bit of a sore head." She prayed that he couldn't smell the scent of alcohol on her breath, which also stunk like Dot Cotton's ashtray.

"Well, I'll make a cuppa for us now," he said giving her a warm, wonderful kiss.

Mari smiled like a satisfied cat. So far, so good! Tim

got up slowly from the bed and she noticed he was wearing his underpants and a T-shirt. His boxers, grey pinstripe, were very tasteful, thankfully. She never liked men in Y-fronts. It reminded her too much of her dad's baggy blue pants. She watched Tim pulling on his jeans. Wow! He was really tall – 6'5" at least! She tried not to perv but noticed that although he was slim, his shoulders were nice and broad.

"Milk and sugar?" Tim asked as he leaned over to kiss her again.

"Milk and half a sugar, please," she smiled at him, hoping last night's mascara wasn't a crusty mess on her face.

As soon as he'd left the room, Mari got up and ran to the small mirror that hung on the wardrobe. A young confused looking girl stared back at her. Her green eyes looked tired and her hair was a Sideshow Bob fright wig. Her mascara, as she'd suspected, had dried under her eyes in a sooty mess. She reached for a tissue from her jeans pocket and started to rub her face vigorously. No make-up was better than old make-up.

She jumped back into bed and her sore head sank gratefully into the pillow. She had to be more careful the next time she went out for a drink. He could have been a psycho or something. If her mum knew she'd gone home with a stranger, she'd have had a fit! Anyway, she needn't worry, Tim seemed quite normal. She reached for her mobile phone from her bag and saw a text message waiting for her. It was Helen. "Oi, slapper, when RU coming home? And who was the hunk from last night?! H xx"

She texted back quickly before he came back with the tea. "Haven't done anything but sleep! He's lovely. Back in a bit. M xx"

Mari didn't want to outstay her welcome in case Tim got sick of her. She'd have the cuppa and then she'd go home and wait for him to call for another date. Yes, good plan. Tim came back into the room holding two mugs of tea.

"After we've had these, shall we go to the caff next door for a fry-up?" Tim asked mischievously. "Something to soak all that Tequila up?"

Mari grinned. It was obvious he didn't regret asking her home last night. She drank her tea and noticed that Tim seemed completely at home in her company, and she felt surprisingly comfortable with him too. There were no awkward silences or embarrassment about last night. Oh God, here she was already falling for a man just because he was nice to her and had made her a cup of tea! She'd go for breakfast with him and then home, before she came across as too keen...

As she ate a massive plateful of bacon, sausage, egg and tinned tomatoes in the greasy spoon, she started to learn more about Tim. He was a clerk for a local solicitor's office but his real ambition was to be a novelist. He had the same taste as her in films – his favourite movie was *Betty Blue* and his favourite band was Blur. Very acceptable, Mari thought. To be honest, he could have been a fan of Celine Dion and an admirer of Kevin Costner films and she'd still fancy him. She didn't think she'd ever fancied someone as much. He had a lovely face – a stunning smile and those eyes, they were amazing. Why did he fancy her, she mused as she watched him paying for their breakfasts at the till.

He was far taller than the other men in the queue and stood out like a piece of fine art amongst some plastic tat. Yes, he was gorgeous. She stopped herself from drooling. Perhaps he was just being nice and she would never hear from him again. When he came back, she'd excuse herself and return to her bedroom at home and obsess a bit about him and pray that he'd text her to meet up again.

"Right," Tim said. "What about a visit to the pub for a few pints? Nothing better than hair of the dog!"

"Well, I look a bit of a state." Mari smiled, thinking the idea was quite appealing but she'd have to tidy herself up a bit. Thank God she had some make-up and a hairbrush in her bag.

"You look lovely," Tim said, ever gallant. "Just a few drinks… Only if you want to of course."

"Well, I'm sure you can persuade me." At last, here was a man who was just like her, who said what he wanted and didn't play games, leaving her at home waiting for a text, which, if she was lucky, would only be sent three days after their last meeting, with her waiting for him like a worried hen wondering when her egg would hatch.

The day sped past as they both discovered the same love for gin and tonic and dark and quiet pubs. And praise be, Tim was also a smoker. Mari couldn't believe that she'd managed to hook such a perfect creation.

It was almost 2am when Tim asked quietly, "Your place or mine?"

"Well, your place is closer," Mari said with a smile. She was itching to show him off to the girls but she also wanted to have hot, slutty sex in private, without Helen or Sara teasing her the next morning for being a slapper.

As she climbed the stairs to his flat, Mari laughed as she realised she hadn't been home yet. "I'm like that bloke in *The Man Who Came to Dinner*," she said as Tim pulled her into the flat.

"No. I want you to be here," Tim smiled, recognising the reference immediately.

"'Well, I'll have to go home tomorrow." Mari told him. "I'll need a shower and some clean underwear!"

"Well, we could always have a shower together now."

Bloody hell! She hadn't shaved her legs for a few days. Would he notice? And what about the cellulite on her bum? But the alcohol that flowed through her veins gave her confidence. "Any excuse to see me naked, Tim?"

"Of course," he smiled as he started to strip in front of her. Mari got undressed too and noticed his blue eyes greedily explore her body. Luckily, she'd worn her sexy pink lace bra and knicker set from Marks's that matched for once.

She'd never showered with a man before. To be honest, she had so many hang-ups about her body, that she hadn't found the idea appealing until now. As his hard body pressed against her and the warm water cascaded down her breasts, she knew she'd definitely have sex with him now; she couldn't play hard to get.

She knew he felt the same way as he kissed her passionately. She felt his hands between her legs and she shuddered with pleasure as he made love to her. For the first time ever, she reached orgasm with barely any foreplay. It further reinforced her belief that Tim really was the man for her.

They made love several times that night and Mari knew she was falling hard for Tim as he slept soundly beside her. She prayed he felt the same.

The next morning, she woke up and realised that Tim wasn't by her side. Shit! Was he regretting their night together already? Had her performance been adequate? After all, it was obvious he was very experienced in bed. She grabbed her mobile hoping Helen and Sara weren't too worried about her. There were three texts asking where she was. She sent them both a hurried text, "Sorry, stayed over AGAIN at Tim's. Back later – promise! M x"

Tim came into the bedroom with a cuppa for her. He smiled at her and said, "Last night was mindblowing, Mari."

Mari blushed, pleased that she'd passed the test and said quickly, "I'm not usually that slutty on a first date…"

"Me neither," Tim laughed. "But no regrets." They both sat on the bed and Tim turned the TV on. An old back and white movie was playing and Mari clocked immediately it was an old Bette Davis film. "Look what's on. *The Man Who Came to Dinner!* Tim laughed and pulled her towards him.

Tim and Mari started seeing each other seriously, and for the first month everything was perfect. Helen and Sara had liked him immediately and Mari spent several evenings a week in his company. One evening whilst they were watching, *Jacob's Ladder* on dvd in Tim's flat, Mari noticed that he was very quiet.

"You OK?" Mari asked hesitantly.

Tim turned to face her and said quietly. "Listen, Mari. I've been wanting to tell you something for a while."

Oh shit! What now? Was he married? Did he have kids? Was he gay? No that wasn't possible, not with his sex drive! She should have known there'd be something.

What was wrong with him? She steeled herself, ready for the big reveal. She knew from the expression on his face that it wouldn't be anything positive.

"I didn't want to tell you straight away. But I feel that our relationship could get serious and I don't want to hide anything from you." He reached for her hand and squeezed it gently.

"You can tell me anything," Mari said, trying to be supportive. *Yes, anything apart from the fact that you've got a house full of kids and a fetish for women's underwear...*

"I'm...I'm a manic depressive, Mari. And I have to take some pretty strong medication to keep it under control."

Mari sighed with relief. It could be worse. She didn't know much about manic depression, only that Vivien Leigh, her favourite actress had suffered from this affliction, and that, after 25 years of passion, had driven the love of her life, Laurence Olivier, into another woman's arms.

"I'm glad you told me," Mari said slowly. She knew she had to deal with this in a sensitive way, as it was obvious that Tim was really worried about her reaction to his news. "I don't know much about the... erm... your illness, but it doesn't change the way I feel about you."

Tim stood up and started to pace to and fro, obviously struggling with his emotions.

"The doctor diagnosed me when I was 16," he

explained quietly. "Mum and Dad didn't understand why I was so unstable; one minute hyper and the next minute really down… I had to leave uni when I was 20 and I spent 6 months in the loony bin… It was a really shitty time."

Loony bin! Fuck! Mari thought to herself. Was she seeing a psycho? But she stopped herself from thinking these negative thoughts. She was better than that. She had to be supportive. After all, he seemed completely fine now.

"But your medication's keeping it under control?"

"Most of the time," Tim nodded, obviously more relaxed now he could talk about his illness. "I just wanted to warn you that's all. Lithium is a really strong drug. They have to monitor my bloods…"

"Is there a cure?" Mari asked hopefully.

Tim laughed bitterly. "No, I just have to live with it. And if you want to be a part of my life, I'm afraid that you have to live with it too."

Mari got to her feet and walked towards him. She hugged him tightly. "Tim, I think the world of you and I don't give a shit about the manic depression. We're really happy together and nothing's going to change that."

Tim smiled at her sadly and kissed her lightly. "I just wanted to warn you. Things went tits up with my ex… because of the illness. I just wanted you to know the facts before things got too serious between us."

"Well, I'm really happy with how things are going at the moment." Mari smiled, trying to raise his spirits. "And if you're happy…well, we'll take one day at a time…"

Tim laughed and kissed her again. 'I'm so lucky that I've met you Mari. I think the world of you.' As he embraced her, Mari realised that she was in love with Tim. No stupid illness would ever come between them…

It was October and she and Tim had been an item for eight months. Mari had been the best girlfriend possible, taking him to his appointments in Bridgend to check his blood and ensuring he ate well and cut down on the booze. She'd been researching his illness online and realised that it was a lot more serious than she'd originally thought. When she shared the news with Helen and Sara, they'd both looked concerned, so she didn't say anything else. She didn't tell anyone that she and Tim hadn't had sex for two months, that he was drinking more than ever and that he'd quit his job and worked as a barman in one of the wildest nightclubs in town.

She didn't mention either that his moods had got a lot worse over the last weeks. His bright blue eyes would cloud into grey when the depression hit him and she couldn't do anything to help. She tried to be as patient and understanding as she could but everything reached a head on her 32nd birthday.

She'd arranged for them both to go out for a romantic meal in the Bay and she'd brought a lovely dress for the occasion. She'd arranged with Tim that he'd come and pick her up from home at seven so they could have a drink before the meal. He'd been very quiet that week and Mari hoped a night out would lift his spirits.

She sat in her living room in her new finery drinking a glass of Cava with Helen and Sara, waiting for Tim to turn up. By half past seven, she'd had enough waiting for him and decided to call his mobile. She let the phone ring for ages until it clicked into answerphone. She kept her voice light as she left a message, "Hi, it's me. Just checking you remember about tonight. The table's booked for eight. Sure you're on your way… Ta-ra."

She could see Sara and Helen looking at her worriedly. *Shit! Where was he?* He knew she'd been looking forward to this for ages. She was always early for every appointment and hated being late. The hours dragged by horribly slowly and by ten o'clock she realised he wasn't coming.

"Listen," Sara said quietly. "Perhaps he's…you know… because of the illness… Leave him be and I'm sure he'll ring you tomorrow. Come out with us tonight so we can celebrate your birthday together."

"Yes, there's no point ruining your birthday," Helen added.

Mari reached for her phone. "No, the illness isn't an excuse. He's a selfish bastard and he knew very well I was looking forward to tonight. Twat!" She left another message on his answerphone that expressed her feelings perfectly, "Well, thanks a lot, Tim, for ruining my birthday. And I don't care if you're a schizo or a nutter, the least you could do is ring me and tell me you can't come over – twat!'

Mari turned to her friends. "Right, pass that Cava over. Now!" Helen passed the bottle over without saying a word.

The following evening, Mari knocked on Tim's door, still fuming. He still hadn't got in touch with her and she knew he wasn't at work as she'd just called in there to see if he was around. But they hadn't seen him either. When the door opened, he stood there like a statue, with huge shadows under his listless eyes. He hadn't shaved and he looked awful.

"There you are!" Mari pushed passed him into the flat. "I thought you'd died or something! Where were you last night?" She turned to face him, her eyes flashing with anger.

"Listen, Mari, I'm really sorry, but I feel awful… This depression… I just couldn't face going out… I'm sorry."

"Sorry? Why didn't you ring me for God's sake! I could have come over to see you instead! This illness doesn't give you carte blanche to be a selfish dick you know! I didn't see that in the list of symptoms!

Mari felt a bit better now she'd had a chance to vent. She waited for his response. Tim looked at her for a long time and said quietly, "If you feel like that, well, I don't want to be a burden."

"Oh, that's it, is it? You're giving up because I gave you a bollocking? That's convenient!" She sat on the bed and frowned at him. She wasn't going anywhere. She wanted the old Tim, the loving and sexy Tim, not the weird and distant Tim that stared at her with a stranger's eyes.

Tim sat beside her on the bed and held her hand. "Listen Mari, do you think I like feeling like this? Feeling like everything's closing in on me? I just couldn't see you last night! I couldn't function in any way. I couldn't pick up the phone, couldn't escape from this prison of a room. You just don't understand!"

"No, I don't understand!" Mari shouted. "I do my best to understand but how can I if you don't let me help you? We'll go back to the doctor, get him to change your pills… There has to be something we can do!" The tears were running down her cheeks and feelings were a mess. She loved him but she hated him too. She just wanted them to be happy. Why couldn't they be happy?

"I can't change things. I have to wait until I feel better, that's all… That's how things are… I'm really sorry."

Mari looked into his eyes as she thought about what to say next. She loved him, she loved him so much. She couldn't finish it with him. She'd have to help him through it, there was nothing else for it…

Things got better after their big fight and Mari tried her best to be patient with Tim, although he didn't keep to any pre-arranged date and the sex situation was hopeless. Mari tried to ignore the strain of feeling that she was walking on egg shells until she happened to call at the flat (by this time, she was trusted with a key), to find Tim unconscious on the bed with an empty bottle of vodka and some pills beside him.

He had been lucky this time, the Doctor told her, matter of factly, but he emphasised that Tim needed to see his psychologist regularly.

As she stood at Tim's bedside in the hospital, Mari felt a wave of love towards him. She couldn't leave him like this, she had to be strong for both of them. She stroked his forehead lightly. He looked so young and peaceful in his sleep. She hoped with all her heart that he'd agree to go back to the shrink. He needed help and in time he'd be OK again. This was just a blip, wasn't it? After all, millions of people lived normal lives and dealt with this illness. Didn't they?

Suddenly Helen and Sara burst in to the room like two hurricanes. "Mari, are you OK. How's Tim?" Sara asked, her eyes like saucers.

"He's OK," Mari whispered. "They pumped his stomach and he's sleeping now."

"Why did he do such a thing?" Helen asked looking at Rob in a combination of anger and disbelief.

"He's ill Helen. He can't help what he did,"

"I understand that, Mari," Helen said, reaching out to take her hand. "Where are his parents?"

"I didn't want to worry them and I don't think Tim would want them to know…"

"It's too much for you to deal with on your own. You're not his mum," Sara said giving her a hug.

"He's only got me. And I'd be a bitch to finish with him because he's ill. I love him, Sara!"

"I know, but you have to put your health first. Look, your nerves are shot. I don't remember when I last saw you laugh… You can't rescue him; you've tried. You have to take care of yourself. You're not his mum or his psychiatrist. It's only Tim that can help himself out of this situation… And the important thing is that he doesn't make you happy anymore… And you'll make yourself sick too if you don't watch out."

"Sara, we've discussed this and you know I'm not going to leave Tim. He needs help that's all and then he'll be fine…"

"Will he?" Helen asked. "What if he succeeds next time? What if you don't get there in time? What will you do then?"

"Shush!" Mari said trying to keep her voice down. "You don't understand! I love him and I'm not going to abandon him because he's ill!"

"No-one would blame you…"

"You better go." Mari turned her back on her two friends and held Tim's hand tenderly.

Sara and Helen shared a look of hopelessness as they left the room reluctantly.

Mari didn't know what to say to him after the *incident*. Tim didn't want to discuss it and his eyes flashed with pain if she tried to reason with him and persuade him to see his psychiatrist. But a wall had come up between them and there was no way to bring it down. Mari was doubtful that the well Tim, the Tim she'd fallen in love with, would ever come back.

A month later and Mari was worried what she'd find every time she called on Tim. She decided to confide in Sara over a bottle or two of wine one night after spending a day tidying Tim's flat – in an attempt to raise his spirits and improve on the so called Feng Shui in his dingy and messy flat.

"You have to think about yourself, Mari. His illness is making you ill too!"

But Mari was determined to make this relationship work. She'd never felt so much for a man as she'd felt for Tim. Together, they'd get through it. Neither Sara nor Helen had experienced a love like this and they just couldn't understand it.

Back to the present

Shit! She'd just run someone over! Oh my God! Was he dead? She couldn't tell from here. She'd be some Hairy Mary's bitch in *Prisoner Cell Block H*, now, and it was all Tim's bloody fault! She got out of the car shaking all over and saw this poor guy lying and groaning by the side of the road. Thank God, he was alive at least, Mari thought as she leant over him timidly. Oh fuck! It was Owen! He kept popping up in her life every two years or so like a bloody cuckoo...

"Mari?" Thank God, he obviously wasn't brain damaged as he recognised her too! *Thank sweet baby Jesus he was OK!*

"Yes, oh my God, Owen, I'm so sorry! Have you broken something? Do you want me to call an ambulance?"

"No, I think I'm OK, just a bit of a shock that's all and my knee's killing me..."

Owen got up slowly and painfully, looking at his bike which had suffered the brunt of the impact.

"I'm really sorry, Owen," Mari said, thanking her guardian angel that he was in one piece. She started to babble. "I was so upset that I didn't see you... I'll buy you a new bike... You're not going to take me to court are you? I've got nine points on my license already!"

"No, but I think you should take me for a drink to get over the shock."

Thank God he was a reasonable bloke, Mari thought to herself as she took Owen's arm and escorted him to the nearest pub.

Owen

Ms MILF, 2006

The way Owen had met up with Rhian was unorthodox to say the least. He'd been shopping at the Tesco Metro in Roath, trying to decide between the lazy option, ready-made pizza, or something more adventurous, such as a tomatoey pasta dish, when he clocked her. A girl in her late twenties, pretty without being "showy" as Huw would put it. She was tall and slim with lovely curly auburn hair around her heart-shaped face with the cutest freckles on her cheeks. She was pushing a trolley and sadly for him, sat inside was a "mini-me" version of her – a small boy, about two years old with the same auburn curls and a cheeky expression on his face.

Owen smiled in a fatherly way at the kid, but the cheeky little bastard stuck his tongue out in response. *Kids!* It was obvious the little runt was suffering from ADHD or something Owen thought scornfully as he watched the boy throwing Wotsits on the floor to his mother's annoyance.

Right, he *was* going to cook tonight – the diet of

kebabs, McDonalds and Subway was surely going to lead to an ulcer or bowel cancer – they had to eat something decent now and again. He decided on spag bol', easy and only two saucepans required. But as he reached for the glass passata bottle, he saw the MILF doing exactly the same thing and as they reached together, the passata bottle fell from their grasp and fell with a loud crack on to the concrete floor. The scene in Tesco was like something out of *Apocalypse Now* with tomato sauce everywhere. Over his trainers, his jeans and even his head!

"Oh, I'm so sorry!" the MILF said rummaging for a packet of wet wipes from her bag and handing them to him. "Don't worry," Owen said courteously, bewitched by her lovely blue eyes and the smattering of freckles on her nose. "It's my fault, I shouldn't have decided on Spaghetti Bolognaise tonight… If I cook, a disaster always happens!" They both laughed at his rather weak joke. Huw would be impressed with him – his repartee was getting better!

But there was another disaster waiting to happen as the young boy (or son of Satan), behind his mother's back, grabbed a bottle of passatta and threw it directly at Owen's feet. It all happened as if by slow-mo; the lovely mother and Owen shouted together: "Nnnnnnnnoooooo! But it was too late. The tomato bomb had ignited and Owen's expensive Nike trainers and beloved Diesel jeans, already critically injured from the first blow, had paid the price with their material lives.

"Harry!" The MILF scolded her charge. "What did you do?"

The boy stared slyly at Owen for a moment before starting to cry. *The little git!* He knew exactly what he was doing – his actions had been deliberate – damn him! One of Tesco's automatons come towards them carrying a mop like a martyr.

"We're so sorry," the MILF said as she tried to pick the pieces of glass that surrounded them.

"Watch your hands," the Tesco bloke said abruptly as he started to mop up around them.

Owen and the MILF shared a "What's his problem?" look, and she whispered, "Look, your trainers and jeans are ruined. If you give me your details, I'll send you a cheque."

Surreptitiously Owen checked her left hand and was pleased to see that she wasn't married. "No you don't have to pay for them, accidents happen. But it might be a good idea for me to take your details anyway, just in case. I can check the next time you and Harry are in Tescos so that I can wear some overalls!"

Zing! He was on fire! She laughed and gave him a business card. He read quickly, "Rhian Mai, PR Co-ordinator, Eco Ltd."

Eco? The name rang a bell – Cardiff's new environmental agency. He smiled at her again. "I'm

Owen. Well, it was…nice to meet you both. I'll give you a call."

She smiled and Owen felt the strength of the attraction between them instantly. As he walked home, his clothes covered with tomato pulp, he thought that it might be worth losing a pair of trainers and expensive jeans if the lovely Rhian was the consolation prize.

Three days later and he was ready to make the call. After a discussion with Huw, they decided that three days were perfect – not too desperate but not too nonchalant either. As Huw said, "These things are very delicate…the first call, you have to weigh all the factors carefully…"

"Factors?" Owen asked as he paced to and fro in their living room with his mobile phone, trying to find the bravery and chutzpah to make the call.

"Yes, the timing – not too early in case she thinks you're some freak that gets up really early, but not before lunch because everyone's tetchy then because they're hungry, and not too late at night in case she thinks you're a stalker!"

"You overthink everything Huw! I'm going to ring her now, OK!"

Huw studied his watch like a scientist looking at a specimen under the microscope. 3 o'clock. Well, it could be better, could be worse…"

But Owen's trembling hands were already dialling the

number on the business card. He hoped in a way that she wouldn't pick up so he could leave a cool and laidback message on her answerphone. But no, after three rings, she answered.

"Hello, Rhian Mai speaking."

Owen shivered as he heard her bright and friendly voice. Shit, what was he doing! What if she said no? What if she didn't remember him? He walked out of the living room and into his bedroom, so Huw couldn't listen to the conversation and then give him a mauling like a Pop Idol judge.

'Oh, hiya Rhian…erm…it's Owen here, the bloke who got a tomato shampoo from Harry the other day in Tescos?"

Yes, good so far, light and easy and he was bound to win brownie points for remembering the name of her horrid son. He heard her lovely tinkling laughter on the phone.

"Oh, hi Owen, how are things? How are your war wounds?"

"Well, I'm still suffering from post-traumatic stress disorder, but I'm having some therapy."

She laughed again – my God! He was on form today. He was making Peter Kay himself look like Jim Davidson!

Right, it was important for him to go in for the kill now before she got fed up with his quips. This was his chance, his only chance to reel her in!

"I was wondering, Rhian, if you're not busy that is…

if you'd like to go out for a drink with me Friday night? I just need to go over a few things with you before I take you and Harry to court over the Passata attack…"

"Well… I think I'm free to attend such an important meeting…'

"Great! What about the HA HA! Bar in town at eightish?"

"Yes, looking forward to it."

Heaving a huge sigh of relief, Owen ended the call and skipped back to the lounge adopting the stance of an Olympic champion.

"Well, someone has a hot date with a MILF to look forward to," Huw smiled as he played XBOX in his pants on the sofa.

"Ugh! MILF, it's such a crude term…"

"*Mother I'd like to Fuck*," Huw said. "Does what it says on the tin. Anyway, when's the big date?"

"Well, a casual drink to start, next Friday."

"Very sensible. If things go well and she's not boring or a madwoman, then you can take her out for a meal and then more drinks…"

"I don't think she'll be boring or a madwoman," Owen said thoughtfully as he gripped the joystick and joined Huw in a Lara Croft adventure.

"You never know, Owen. What about Damien?" Huw asked as he let Lara strike Owen's soldier with a monster sword.

"Who?"

"Spawn of the Devil… That kid of hers!"

"Well, he's not coming out Friday night is he? No, he's OK, just a bit high spirited that's all. I'm sure he'll love his Uncle Owen once I've bribed him with sweeties."

"You can't win a kid's love with bribes you know. Kids can spot a fake a mile away." Huw, now in teacher mode, nodded sagely.

"Well, I'll cross that bridge when I come to it, if things develop," Owen said, his voice a lot more confident than his real feelings. He was in the big league now – a mother and child, not the flibbertigibbet youngsters he'd been dallying with in the past few years, following his lucky escape from cougar, Maggie Lewis. Rhian was different – she had responsibilities – a real flesh and blood child. The question was, would Owen be man enough for her?

A month later, Owen felt confident that Rhian was his perfect woman. She was clever, funny, mature and very, very sexy. The only buzzing bluebottle in the soup was that little shit of a son of hers, Harry. Even though he was only three, the little rascal knew exactly how to drive Owen crazy. On his first visit to their home, he threw some baked beans on Owen's new Paul Smith shirt! He'd also driven his little "Noddy" car over his shoeless feet. And on one occasion, he'd vomited all over the back seat of Owen's new car! Owen felt he deserved an Oscar for his low-key and understanding response to this endless catalogue of misdemeanours.

"Oh Harry!" Rhian would sigh as she mopped up the mess. Harry would smirk at Owen knowingly. Owen was trapped – he couldn't show his anger towards the infant, he was only a child, even if he was a devil child. Owen was ready to tolerate the boy for Rhian's sake.

He hadn't asked her much about her "ex-", he preferred to imagine that "Jim" didn't exist; that Rhian had experienced an immaculate conception and not had an intense relationship that had spawned a child.

It was obvious that Rhian didn't want to talk about him either. Owen sensed that ending the relationship hadn't been easy for her either and apart from mentioning that Harry was away with his dad, Jim, during the weekend, she didn't mention him at all.

Owen loved the weekends for that reason. Now he had Rhian to himself. He wondered if he could persuade her to pack the brat off to boarding school when he was old enough for kindergarten. Didn't Stephen Fry mention on TV that he'd been sent to boarding school at the tender age of five or something?

Anyway, it was a marvellous Saturday – Harry was with his dad and Owen and Rhian were free to have hot and noisy sex in Owen's bedroom. Huw was out of the way in his room, watching *Bottom* dvds on a loop and Owen had the prettiest girl in the world lying naked in his arms. And in the corner of the room, sat the second prettiest girl in the world – his new guitar, the Fender Stratocaster in Sunburst Brown. Yes, the magical Strat that he'd ordered especially online from the US. And had waited two months for it to arrive. Even though he'd given up the band when he left uni, he was still really into his music and had always wanted a Strat since he was a kid. And after a lot of saving and sacrifice, she was his at last.

"Owen?" Rhian jumped on top of him mischievously.

"Mmm?" His eyes were still stroking the new guitar lovingly.

"You can play with your new toy later. I'm number one now!"

"Sorry," Owen laughed and pulled her towards him for a kiss.

He was going through his usual repertoire of sexual moves when he heard a deafening knock on the front door. He continued to make love with Rhian, after all, Huw could answer the door…

After a few minutes just as Owen was about to climax, he heard loud voices in the sitting room and then heavy footsteps running up the stairs like a herd of wildebeest. *What the fuck?* His body froze in fear.

"What's wrong?" Rhian murmured, still lost in the moment.

"I'm not sure," Owen whispered. "Burglars?"

"Don't be daft! Burglars don't make that kind of racket. Must be some noisy friends of Huw's," Rhian said casually. "Don't stop, I'm really close."

"Your wish is my command, madam!" Owen said.

But as he continued to make love to Rhian, the bedroom door opened unceremoniously. Bloody Huw, what did he want now? But then Owen clocked the look on Rhian's face –it was a combination of fear and anger. Was Huw in his Homer Simpson underpants again? He'd warned him about frightening Rhian with his bizarre choice of undergarments.

But no, as he turned to look, he could see a huge stranger standing there scowling at them both. He was the spitting image of the footballer turned actor, Vinnie Jones, if not more muscular and threatening looking. What the hell? He pulled himself awkwardly away from Rhian and his voice shook slightly, "Who are you and what the fuck are you doing in my bedroom?"

By now, Huw had stepped gingerly into the room with two middle-aged guys following him sheepishly. Huw coughed delicately and looked at the Vinnie Jones look alike with pure fear in his eyes. "Owen, sorry, but he burst in with these two private detectives… I couldn't stop them."

By now, Rhian had pulled the quilt around her and was screaming like a banshee. "What the fuck are you doing here, Jim?"

Jim...? Oh shit, Jim was her ex's name.

"What the fuck are *you* doing here?" Jim barked back. "We've only been separated for six months and here you are whoring around with this twat here!"

"Hey!" Owen tried to find a shred of bravery from somewhere. "I'm not a twat, OK, and you should go before I call the cops!"

"Erm boys... Cup of tea?" Huw asked the two detectives desperately. They nodded and the three of them shuffled awkwardly out of the bedroom.

Rhian ignored them and turned her attentions to Jim angrily. "Yes, Jim. We've finished. You can see Harry anytime you want, but we're over, you know that."

"You don't give a shit about Harry. He's told me that you only have time for this bloke now!" Jim spat at her.

"Jim, he's three years old. I doubt very much that he told you anything about Owen."

"You're a bloody psycho you know that? Who hires a private detective, a mentalist that's who!"

"But I had to know what you were doing, in case Harry was in harm's way," Jim said.

"You know that Harry is my main priority and I'd never harm him! This is jealousy, pure and simple and nothing more! Well, now you know what I've been doing so we don't need to discuss this any further. So get out!"

"Yeah, you better go, mate," Owen said with an air of quiet authority.

"You shut your fucking mouth," Jim yelled, his temper now approaching the top of the Richter scale as he walked towards the bed with his fists ready to strike Owen.

"No, Jim, don't!" Rhian screamed.

Jim froze for a few seconds like a cartoon character with his fist suspended in mid air. And then he looked wildly around the room before his gaze landed on Owen's new guitar. Owen noticed this immediately and started to pray, *not the Strat, please God, not the Strat.*

"Jim!" Owen tried to calm him like a circus lion tamer with a particularly ferocious beast. "You can smack me if it'll make you feel better…but please, don't harm the guitar… It's a brand new Stratocaster…"

But as he uttered those last three words, it was too late. Jim was like some deranged wrestler and had lifted the guitar above his head and was striking it against the bedroom wall.

Owen couldn't watch and with yelping with pain, he buried his head in the pillow. Rhian stood up awkwardly, still wrapped in the duvet. "Jim, you better go, Owen's flatmate will be calling the cops any minute now."

Jim stared at her, his eyes full of anger and pain. Slowly, he dropped the sorry remains of the Stratocaster onto the floor and walked out of the room without another word.

Rhian sat down on the bed beside Owen with a sigh. "Owen," she said quietly. "Owen?"

176

"He's destroyed the g… my Strat…" He closed his eyes, unable to look at the devastation.

"I'm so sorry, Owen," Rhian stroked his hair gently. "I'll pay for a new guitar for you."

"But it won't be the same," Owen murmured, his heart about to break with the loss.

"Listen, Jim's an OK guy really and a great father. He just hasn't come to terms yet with the fact that we've finished, that's all."

"You think?" Owen said.

"I think he understands now, about us," Rhian said consolingly. "And I'm sure this won't happen again."

"There's nothing left to break, anyway,' Owen said sadly.

"Listen, Owen, the Strat isn't the issue!" Rhian barked, fed-up with his dramatics about the guitar. "I'll buy you a new one!"

Owen got up and grabbed his clothes and started to dress clumsily. "You're right, Rhian," he said quietly as he came to a swift decision in his head. "The guitar isn't the issue. The issue is that you've got a psycho ex-boyfriend who's still in your life and who bursts in here willy-nilly with private detectives to spy on us whilst we're…at it! That's the issue! And to be honest with you, I think your life is way too complicated for me. I'm a simple guy. I like guitars, films, drinking San Miguel, playing Xbox… I don't want to be a part of some weird soap-opera!"

"What are you saying, Owen? You're going to give up on us just like that over this one little episode? I thought we had a chance together…" Rhian got up and started to get dressed too.

"I really like you, Rhian." He was starting to have doubts – his heart started to melt – she looked so sexy in her white frilly bra and knicker set. "But a crazy ex- who breaks in here, almost assaults me and then destroys the most valuable thing I have, in the company of two private detectives, well, that's not a 'little episode' in my book!'"

"I really like you, too, Owen. Jim knows the score now. We won't have any more trouble from him, I promise. In time, he'll understand that he's still a key part of Harry's life but that he can't be a part of our lives.'

Owen felt a shiver of fear as he heard her saying the words, "our lives." God, he'd only been seeing the woman for five minutes and she was already talking about them as a "unit" as "us". Another few months and he'd be walking around Ikea like a zombie trying to decide between a Noddy or Snoopy bedset for Harry. No, he was way too young for this kind of responsibility. He was also too immature to deal with a scary ex- and the spawn of Satan… He turned to face Rhian. "I don't think we should keep seeing each other. It's just too complicated."

"This isn't about Jim at all is it?" Rhian let go of his hand as if he had some kind of contagious disease. "It's because I have a kid, that's the real reason you want to finish isn't it?"

"Yes and no. Jim will always be part of your life because of Harry and I understand that. But Harry hates me Rhian and I don't think I'm ready to take on a ready made family…"

"Harry loves you!"

"No, he hates me and I dislike him," Owen said bluntly, feeling a strange relief that he could be honest for once.

He clocked the shock in her eyes as she absorbed that little bombshell.

"What? But I thought you liked Harry!"

"No I like *you*, Rhian. I don't really like kids that much…not at the moment anyway…not other people's."

"But you tolerate him because of me," Rhian finished the sentence for him.

Owen didn't answer. He looked at the floor instead.

"Well, I can't force you to love my child and we come as a unit." Rhian grabbed her handbag and walked towards the door.

As she left, she turned to look at the sorry remains of the guitar, "I wouldn't worry too much about that being broken. After all, you're no Eric Clapton are you?"

And with that, she slammed the door with a loud bang and left.

Owen sat on the floor stroking the guitar's remains

gently. He would send Rhian the bill the next morning. The least she could do is pay for a new one as she'd promised. Otherwise, he'd get the cops involved and get that Jim to cough up. If she hadn't trashed his guitar playing skills, he would have gone to Jim first, but she had no right to say he was a crap guitarist – she hadn't even heard him play, not on stage, anyway. She would pay for that slight.

This was the last time he'd pick a woman with "baggage". From now on, it would be single ladies only – no kids, no drama and no mad exes.

"You OK, pal?" Huw popped his head round the door.

"No thanks to you, you twat! Why the fuck did you let them in?"

"I didn't have any choice! They'd pushed their way past me before I had a chance to stop them!"

"Well, Rhian and I are over and the fucking psycho wrecked my Strat, too!"

"Shit!" Huw pondered for a minute as he surveyed the damaged guitar. "Well, why don't you go the offie and get us a bottle of JD or something – for the shock." He put his arm around his friend's shoulders. "I'll get on the blower and order us a nice soothing pizza with all the trimmings."

As he cycled to the off licence, Owen replayed the night's crazy events. What was wrong with him? He had a frightening talent for choosing the wrong girl, he did it time after time. Why couldn't he be like Huw and pick a normal girl like Elin.

As he turned on to Albany road, Owen saw a car coming towards him like a bat out of hell. Shit, surely it would see him, he had his lamp on. But no, before he could take any evasive action, the car had clipped him and knocked him off the bike. He landed with a sickening thud on the edge of the pavement. *Ooof!* Was he alive? He was. *Oh my God, the pain, the pain!* Was he in one piece?

His knee hurt like hell, but nothing was missing. And at least the car had stopped. Where was the bloody fool that had run him over? But before he had a chance to see who was leaning over him, everything went dark.

"Owen! Owen!" He could hear a faraway voice calling him insistently. Slowly, he opened his eyes and focused on the worried face hovering over him. No way! It couldn't be! It was Mari, that girl from Reel-Time – she'd run him over! Oh my God, the world was laughably small!

"Oh my God, Owen, I'm so sorry. Did you break anything? Shall I call an ambulance?"

He could see that her pretty face was tear strewn and that her hands were shaking as she stroked his hair gently. He softened immediately as he tried to reassure her.

"No I think I'll be OK. Just a shock that's all. And my knee's killing me…'

He got up slowly and painfully and took a quick look at his bike that had taken the worst of the hit. Typical! No guitar and now no bike. That's all he needed. Another girl must be due round the corner to kick him in the nuts and complete this shittiest of evenings.

"I'm so sorry, Owen. I was really upset about something, I just didn't see you… I'll pay for a new bike, I promise. You're not going to take me to court are you? I've got nine speeding points on my licence already!"

Owen looked at her again and was taken aback by her beauty. This might be his chance to get off with her at last!

"No, of course not. But I think you should take me for a stiff drink to get over the shock!" He smiled at her as he tried to ignore the pool of blood that was staining his jeans' leg thanks to his knee injury.

"But don't you need stitches?" Mari said as she clocked the blood.

"Nah, just a scratch," Owen lied. He could get the knee sorted later. This was his chance to have a drink with the elusive Mari!

They decided to call in at The George – which was the closest drinking hole to the scene of the crime, bearing in mind Owen was having difficulty walking. Mari ordered him a triple whisky and sat down beside him. She necked her G and T almost in one gulp. "Medicinal," she told him with a smile.

"So why were you driving like Mr Bean down Albany Road, eh?' Owen asked.

"God, long story," Mari said rolling her eyes. "I'd just finished with my boyfriend and I was so upset, I just wasn't thinking straight. I'm so sorry, I could have killed you."

"Who? That guy you were in the cinema with when we saw *Run Lola Run*?' Owen perked up at this, it meant her engagement was most definitely off.

"Erm no, I finished with him last year... This was another guy." Mari looked a bit embarrassed but he couldn't pick faults, he'd been going through girlfriends like a dose of salts, too. They hadn't found the right person that's all. Perhaps them bumping into each other over the years, literally this time, was some kind of sign or omen? Nah, he didn't believe in omens, did he? He attempted to lighten Mari's mood as she seemed to be on a bit of a downer, understandable as she'd had a shitty night too.

"Well, I wasn't concentrating a 100 per cent either. I finished with my girlfriend tonight, too."

"Oh, what happened with you? Or is it too personal?" Mari lit up a fag and offered him one. Their hands touched as he lit her cigarette for her and he could feel the electricity between them. *God, he really fancied this girl!*

"No, not really, I had an audience after all. Her ex-husband turned up whilst we were… getting intimate… you know. And not only that, he had two private detectives with him as well!"

"Oh my God! Well, my break-up wasn't that dramatic. My ex- is a manic-depressive and I just couldn't deal with it… It had been coming to an end for a while. I've learnt two valuable lessons tonight, Owen. One, don't go out with a guy with baggage and two, drive safely! I think I'll have a break now from blokes, I'm really crap at picking a decent one. I'm going to focus on my career for once!"

"Yeah, I think it'd be a good idea for me to take a breather too," Owen said, although he was itching to lean over and snog the face off Mari. But he could sense she was still obviously fragile after her fresh break-up. He'd bide his time.

"You still working for Celt TV?" Owen asked.

"Yeah, still trying to pitch programmes to dozy Commissioners," she laughed.

"Well, if there's a job going, let me know. I've had a gut full of Farmers' Weekly. If I see yet another pastoral montage of farmyard animals, I'm going to go mental!"

"There is a job going with us: Assistant Producer," Mari said. "Listen, I'll put in a good word for you with the boss; just send me your CV." She scribbled her email address on a piece of paper. "After your near death experience, thanks to my shit driving, it's the least I can do."

Owen smiled at her and they clinked their glasses together. His knee felt a bit better, must be the whiskey. Perhaps tonight hadn't been such a disaster after all?

Chapter 7

Mari

Mr Possible?, 2007

"So the girl of your dreams was gay?" Mari laughed as she listened to Owen's story about Michelle and the school renunion over a drink after work. Since he'd landed the assistant producer job at Celt TV three months earlier, Owen and Mari had started going out for a swift drink after work every week or two and a real friendship was blossoming. Mari was so pleased that she'd recommended him for the job – he was a ray of sunshine in her working life and she looked forward to their evening ritual of a swift half (or three) after work. Most of their colleagues were much older than them or married or just plain boring.

"Obviously, after she'd been with me, no other man was good enough for her!" Owen laughed.

"Or you put her off men for life!" Mari chortled.

"Hm, well… Another gin then?" Owen got up on his feet.

"Yes, why not?" Mari said. "It's Friday night after all." As she watched Owen approaching the bar, Mari realised with a start that she actually quite fancied him. She'd thought he was sexy that night she knocked him off his bike but the attraction had intensified as now they were working together she'd got to know his funny and charming personality Owen was different to Mari's usual type – he was tall, quite skinny (she usually preferred more muscle on her men), but he had a very cute face. Lovely freckles on his nose and big dark eyes. His slacker attitude was appealing and his dry humour and of course they had a shared love of films. But she didn't want to rush into anything other than friendship with Owen. His track record with girls was as bad as hers with men. And she didn't think he viewed her as anything more than a friend. After all, would he have shared the story about his school reunion and thwarted passion if he was interested in her romantically?

"So as we're talking about ghosts of ex-es past, did you ever see Gary again?" Owen asked carefully.

"Nah, not a peek. I hope he's happy though," Mari still felt guilty about the way she treated Gary but also extremely relieved at the same time. It had been the right decision, no doubt about it.

"Did your parents get some of the wedding deposit back?"

"Not a penny," Mari said, sadly. "I'd left it too late. There was only a week to go before the big day."

"Not meant to be, Mari. You did the right thing. You still have your freedom."

Mari nodded and looked at him curiously. "What about you? Any luck with the ladies recently? You haven't mentioned a new amour for at least two weeks!" If he was still on the market, she was going to make her move tonight. She really fancied him and if they were both single, why not?

Owen laughed. "Well, I've had a date with this one girl…"

"You don't sound very keen."

"No, she's really fit you know, blonde, sexy but… Well, we don't have much in common. She's not interested in anything apart from fashion and *Hollyoaks*!" Owen sighed.

A-ha! This is where Mari could score a few points over the bimbo. Although she wasn't blonde or sexy, she had a brain.

"Personality and intelligence are more important than peroxide and big boobs, Owen," Mari said.

"I know but my libido keeps overriding my brain. You remember that episode on Seinfeld—"

"—where his head and his penis play chess against each other?"

"Exactly!"

"Yes. Well, remember what happened at the end of that episode – he followed his head and finished with that bimbo!"

"I haven't got to that stage yet," Owen said rueing his wandering eye. "Anyway, why did you finish it with Gary? You never gave me the gory details."

"It's a tedious story. Although Gary was lovely, he was too much of a pushover for me. I don't want a yes man. I want someone with a bit more backbone, someone who can keep me in line!" She looked at Owen. *Someone like you*, she thought to herself.

"Mmm…you girls! You say you want a new man but in reality you want a caveman who'll drag you by your extensions into the cave for a good seeing-to!"

"You're right! Why do you think all the girls fancy Russell Crowe, the caveman for the new millennium? Anyway, you blokes are all the same. You pretend that you want an independent woman with a good brain but what you want is a fit bimbo, like Kelly Brook, on your arm."

"No, not quite," Owen said. 'What we want is Kelly Brook's face and body, and Carol Vorderman's brains!"

"Impossible! And anyway, I read that Carol only got a third in her degree!"

"Still, she's the only brainy woman I can name." Owen drained the last of his pint. "What about another drink?"

Mari necked her gin. She was having such a good time she didn't want the night to end yet.

"Jesus, Mari. Are we on a session or what?" Owen winked at her.

"We are! If you're man enough to keep up with me!" Tonight was turning out to be a blinder.

"Oh God! Why did you persuade me to come here?" Owen said as they both stood in the middle of a load of 30-somethings trying to hold on to their youth. "Boom Box" was a tacky 80s bar in Cardiff city centre. "Owen, we're so in our 30s, now, not 20s – we have to go to a place where we won't look sad and old!" Mari laughed, pissed as a fart by now.

"At least we're not as sad as that bloke in the Miami Vice outfit and mullet!" Owen pointed to a rotund middle-aged man dancing exuberantly to "Thriller".

"Come on Owen, come and dance!" Mari grabbed his hand as "Thriller" ended and Madonna's "Crazy for You" started. "This is my favourite song ever! When I was 16, and trying to pull this bloke in a party, I wanted the DJ to play this for me…"

"Did it work?"

"No, the DJ didn't have the song but I pulled the guy anyway. He was a real loser!"

"He'd have to be if he wasn't nice to you!" Owen said looking deep into her eyes.

What was this? Were they flirting? Before Mari had a chance to explore this thought any further, Owen leant towards her and started to snog her in the middle of the dance floor. It was a lovely kiss – gentle yet passionate.

Mari kissed him back. And as the two melted into each other's arms, Mari forgot about Tim and his manic depression and Gary and the wedding fiasco…

"So, do you want to share a taxi back with me?" she asked as they put their coats on and walked towards the taxi rank in St Mary's street at the end of the night.

"Mari, I better not. Listen, I really like you," Owen said. "But I've had my fingers burnt before having an office relationship and I had to leave because everything went tits up."

"Owen," Mari grinned, trying to hide her discomfort. "I'm not asking for your hand in marriage… Just a bit of fun that's all. 'Friends with Benefits.'" She was surprised at how disappointed she felt at his rejection.

"I know," Owen said awkwardly. "But I promised myself that I wouldn't start a relationship with someone in work again. It's too complicated. And I really enjoy our friendship. I've never had a girl who's a good friend before. And you know my sorry track record with women."

Mari could see he wouldn't be budged. What a shame, she really liked him. But perhaps he was right, life was complicated enough as it was and she didn't want work complications as well. She didn't want to beg and have to face him in work on Monday knowing she'd made a fool of herself. It was obvious he just wanted friendship.

"You're right," Mari said, desperate to get out of there

now. "It's better that we're just good friends. Lot less trouble."

"Yes," said Owen, relieved that she hadn't made a big deal out of it.

"Here's a taxi. See you Monday!" Mari said as breezily as she could, although she felt completely embarrassed.

"Yes, and thanks for tonight, Mari, it was great." Owen kissed her lightly on her cheek.

"No probs," Mari grinned. As she sat in the taxi on the way home, she watched Owen walking striding along the pavement ahead. Yes, he was cute and perhaps things could have worked out between them. But if he didn't feel the same way, well, there was no point brooding over it…

Owen

Miss Red Light, 2007

Owen and Mari hadn't been out for a drink since Boom Box-gate and even though they were still friendly at the office, Owen could feel things weren't quite the same as before. He felt bad about this but he had done the right thing. He couldn't afford to lose another job over a failed office romance and he valued his friendship with Mari too. Still, he did feel slightly awkward in her company now and wished that they hadn't snogged that night.

With time, hopefully their relationship would go back to normal. He needed to take advantage of his single status he mused thoughtfully as he watched Welsh contenders, Glyn and Imogen's antics on *Big Brother*.

"Sorted!" Huw threw a piece of paper onto Owen's lap.

"What?" Owen paused the TV.

"The trip to Amsterdam, mun! I've booked everything. We leave on Friday, back on Monday. We're staying in the Botel – which is a cool hotel in a boat on the canal… All this for £400 including the flight!"

"How many stars does this boat-hotel have?" Huw had a track record of booking terrible hovels. The worst example had been last year's trip to Dublin for the New Year. Huw had found a "bargain". But they'd discovered that this "bargain" was a grubby council house about 10 miles from the city centre with more flies in the bedroom than on an African plain.

"Three stars, thank you!" Huw said with pride. "No skimping this time and the breakfast looks great – whopping platters of ham, eggs, cheese…"

"Yes, well, the food always looks nicer on the internet."

"Listen, you didn't want to make the arrangements yourself, so shut your chops and be grateful that Uncle Huw's Tours, once more, has made all the plans for you!"

"OK, thanks," Owen said. He didn't want Huw ranting at him for half an hour. But if the hotel was a disaster, he'd enjoy telling him "told you so."

"Now then. What about a pint of Amstel for Dutch courage?"

"OK, I'll go to the offie." Owen grabbed his coat. He was really looking forward to this trip. He'd never been to Amsterdam before but he knew it would be amazing. A smorgasbord of dope, beer and girls – and everything legal! It would be a trip to remember.

"Where is this bloody Botel again?"

Owen dodged yet another tram that sped past like a bloody hurricane.

"The map says it's just by Rembrandt Square." Huw peered at his map like an old man staring at his pension book. "Look, it can't be far."

Owen had imagined some kind of baroque wooden barge bobbing gracefully on the waves but when he saw the fabled Botel he was disappointed. It looked like a big white building in a kind of boat shape but without any style or romance. Never mind, at least they were near the action and that was more important than anything.

"See?" Huw said, as they threw their rucksacks onto the two single beds in the room. "Has Uncle Huw done well or has Uncle Huw done well?"

"Uncle Huw's done OK, for once," Owen replied with a grin. "But I'm holding back on my final verdict until I've seen and sampled breakfast."

"Right then. Let's go and scout out these coffee shops. That's where they sell the good stuff."

"OK!"

They left the hotel and walked towards the city centre. But finding the fabled coffee shops wasn't as easy as they'd expected.

"There's one!" Huw would exclaim excitedly, to find there was only pancakes and beer for sale. "Shit!"

They wandered around Amsterdam in increasing frustration at their failed quest. "What about a pint anyway? I'm gasping!" Owen was fed up with the fruitless search for marijuana.

"No, no. Look, here's one! Grandad's Moustache! And look they sell dope!"

They could see a young guy sat in the coffee shop window smoking a huge spliff. They rushed inside like two kids into a sweet shop. The atmosphere was smoky yet sweet and the tiny café was full of personality, decorated with portraits of some of the most famous cigarette and dope smokers in history adorning the tobacco stained walls: Bob Marley, Humphrey Bogart, James Dean and Bette Davis all puffed away enigmatically.

Owen took a casual look at the clientele and was surprised to see a broad cross-section of society enjoying Grandad's Moustache – from young students to dreadlocked cool black guys, to a wrinkled old lady, who resembled his nan, sitting in the corner smoking a huge pipe. There wasn't any food on the menu, but food wasn't the attraction. The big bearded guy behind the counter handed them a huge menu with a long list of different types of cannabis on it and small illustrations by each name. You could buy a spliff ready-rolled or buy the stuff to roll yourself. Huw and Owen had limited rolling skills and after some keen browsing decided on the mildest option, the Green Goddess.

"Wow! This Green Goddess is delicious!" Huw said, sucking deeply on the spliff.

"This is the life, my friend." Owen laughed, already feeling high. "Thank you for organising it."

Two hours later, they were both stoned and extremely hungry. As they left the coffee shop, Huw made a note of the street and shop name on his map, in case it disappeared into the labyrinthian confusion of the city and they couldn't find it again. After munching a bag of falafels that they bought from a cheap and cheerful food stand, they were both ready for a couple of pints.

"We'll have a wee break from the spliffs for a bit," Huw said, "so we don't peak too soon. It's important that we don't overdo things, 'cause we've got three days to go yet!"

"You're quite right," Owen agreed. "We'll break it up a bit and have a pint now instead." After a few pints of Amstel, they were pleasantly toasted and decided to head back to the Botel. It was almost 2am and Owen was knackered. As they wandered through the picturesque De Wallen steets, Owen noticed through an alcoholic fug a strange juxtaposition – on one side of the street, the majestic town buildings, including churches still splendid in their grandeur and directly opposite the shabby "red light" sex shops. Confusing yet apt in a way, Owen mused philosophically – after all sin and redemption went hand in hand.

"Fucking hell!" Huw exclaimed, his eyes like saucers. "Look at this one!"

Owen had been doing his best to avoid looking at the ladies of the night since they'd landed in Amsterdam. This had been the big attraction for Huw, but Owen was more interested in the legal marijuana than picking up an STD or worse. These women stood like vacant dolls in their shop windows; they were dressed in gaudy underwear to tempt in stag night males or repressed husbands for an hour or two. Owen took a quick peek at the girl in the nearest window. She seemed different to the ones he'd already seen. She appeared innocent and sweet, without the empty stare that the other girls had. She was blonde and young, probably only in her early twenties and dressed in a rather ethereal silky negligée rather than the garish, tight synthetic push up bras and G-strings the other girls wore. She had a very pretty face and barely any make-up. She looked like a regal swan amongst some scruffy pigeons.

"What about it?" Huw slurred as he prodded Owen in the ribs. "When in Rome and all that…"

"What? You can't be serious! You want to pay for it? With a prostitute?"

"Ssh!" Huw admonished him. "You don't know who might be listening!"

"It's not illegal here you idiot, so what does it matter? Do you think your mum and dad are hiding around the corner?"

"You never know!" Huw touched his nose with his finger.

"Let's just go back to the Botel, Huw. I don't fancy catching VD from a prostitute!"

"You can use a condom, stupid!"

"It's not my bag, OK!" Owen said decisively, although his beer goggles kept drifting back to the girl in the window. She caught him looking and smiled at him. She was really beautiful, with long blonde hair and a lithe shapely body. And they hadn't had much luck with girls so far this trip. Most of the pretty ones in Amsterdam seemed to be cycling hand in hand with their hipster boyfriends. And Owen hadn't had sex for ages… There ought to be something quite different and exciting about having sex with a professional who knew how to please a man. After all, it had been going on long enough that there must be something in it, especially now when even ordinary girls were up for it when they fancied you. But it was wrong, wasn't it? Paying for sex? It was cheap and nasty and above all, scary. How could he perform effectively with a "pro"? He had enough trouble summoning up the guts to do it with a regular girl. But shouldn't he try it, just this once? And that beautiful girl didn't look like your typical hooker – she might be a newbie. Perhaps he could even rescue her, like Richard Gere in *Pretty Woman*. He scoffed at himself immediately. Shit, he must be pissed to reference a chick flick like that!

Huw sensed his friend was changing his mind, "Listen, it's only a bit of fun and it's quite safe or it wouldn't be 'legit'. We'll go in just to see how much it costs for an hour or so, and if we don't feel comfortable we'll go back to the Botel." And before Owen could stop him, Huw had opened the door and was inside the brothel. Owen followed him reluctantly, though he had to admit he was curious. The place was even more miserable inside than it appeared on the outside. The yellowing walls were tobacco tainted and behind the wooden counter stood a middle-aged peroxide blonde in a short red mini-dress. Behind her, Owen could see an old portable TV playing an 80s porn film. Her face was a stony mask as she lifted her head from her magazine

"Excuse me, how much for one hour?" Huw stumbled over his words.

The woman didn't answer but pushed some sort of menu towards them. Huw opened it and Owen realised it was a list of girls – with photos and corresponding prices. *Shit*, Owen thought as he checked the cost of the beautiful girl in the window. According to the menu, her name was Celeste, she was 21 years old, 34–26–35 and 5 feet 4 inches tall. A natural blonde, she did everything except for S&M he was relieved to read as he didn't fancy being spanked til his buttocks or, worse, his balls bled. He'd seen enough dodgy porn films to see how that little game could go wrong

Huw was in his element studying the menu and he selected a striking black girl, "Ebony", who was 23 years old, 36–28–36 and 5 feet 6 inches tall. She did everything according to the menu.

"120 euros for an hour!" Owen exclaimed. "That's over a £100! You'd think the place would be classier with all the cash they're raking in!"

"Ssh! The lady's getting impatient. Do you want Celeste then?"

"I don't know." Owen could feel his heart beating erratically. He wasn't sure he had the balls to go through with it.

Huw turned to the madam and said, as if ordering two steaks in a restaurant, "I'd like Ebony, please, and my friend would like Celeste, for one hour only."

He turned to Owen. "We don't want any cockups with them asking for more than 120 euros."

"Pay now," the woman said.

"I've got cash." Huw fumbled for his wallet.

Owen looked in his wallet and realised with some relief that he didn't have enough money. "I don't have enough cash," he whispered to Huw.

"Bloody Hell, Owen, I told you to bring plenty of cash with you! Where's your credit card?"

"Back in the hotel. It's for emergencies only, I told you that."

"Well, it's lucky I'm here to pull your chestnuts out of the fire; I've got a card."

"Cash only," the madam said, deadpan. She was obviously used to lads whose eyes were bigger than their wallets.

"You go, Huw, I don't mind, honestly," Owen stammered.

"No, no we both have to do this. I don't want you being all holier than thou tomorrow…"

"You go to the machine," the madam said to Owen, obviously having had enough of them both by now.

"I'll go with him," Huw said.

"Ebony only has one hour. You go to her now and Celeste will go with your friend."

"See you later then, boy…' Huw winked at Owen as he followed the madam up the stairs.

Owen stood awkwardly by the counter until the madam returned a few minutes later. She went into another room behind the counter and a few seconds later reappeared, Celeste following her like a docile lamb. Behind Celeste, a tall, muscular man in his early 30s brought up the rear. He had a blonde crew-cut and wore a well-pressed black suit. He was frighteningly well-built, like Russell Crowe in *Gladiator* and Owen quaked in his boots.

"Celeste and Anthony will take you to machine. Hurry!"

Owen felt as if he was in some kind of surreal dream as he followed Anthony and Celeste through the narrow Amsterdam streets. The city was still heaving with people and the heady scent of beer, food and perfume filled the air. Owen started to feel sick – a combination of fear, dope and Amstel – and lost his balance as he tried to keep up with his companions. Celeste noticed and slowed down to help him. She offered him her arm and asked in broken English, "You okay? You sick?"

"Too much lager!"

"Cashpoint isn't far now," Celeste smiled sweetly at him.

Anthony hadn't said a word but was keeping a close eye on them both. Anthony was obviously the "muscle", ensuring the punters didn't abscond without paying and making sure the girls were safe.

Finally, they reached a cashpoint and with trembling fingers, Owen took out 120 euros from his account. Was he insane? But he'd fallen under Celeste's spell – she was so beautiful and she seemed to like him (although she was paid to do that)… But he did feel a certain chemistry between them or was he kidding himself? She was probably just a really good actress. But it was too late now, he had to pay up or face Anthony's angry fists…

"OK?" the madam nodded at Anthony and Owen handed over the 120 Euro to her with shaking hands Anthony nodded.

"Room 10, Celeste. One hour."

Celeste nodded and offered her hand to Owen and led him up the stairs.

They didn't speak as they walked down the long corridor. Owen wondered where Huw was and if he was up to the job. With the combined effects of the Amstel and dope, Owen was very dubious that Huw could do much no matter how experienced Ebony might be.

"In here," Celeste said as she pulled Owen into the room. It looked like a typical cheap hotel room. In the dim light of a table lamp he made out a double bed with a flowery, though clean looking duvet over it, an old wooden cupboard by the window and a wooden armchair beside it – hardly boutique chic, but at least it looked and smelled clean.

"You relax," Celeste pushed him tenderly on to the bed. Owen lay on the bed awkwardly as Celeste began to strip in front of him. But as he looked at her pert little breasts and her gorgeous body undulating for his pleasure, he noticed that her blue eyes were completely devoid of emotion. She wasn't turned on, she was going through the motions, for him as she did for all the other Johns. It was as if she was in a trance, as if she wasn't in this room with him, not really. He felt his erection shrink and disappear as he realised that this wasn't sexy, it was just sad, a young girl like this selling her body. Worst of all, he was the disgusting punter, taking advantage of her.

"Celeste…" He got up from the bed awkwardly. "I'm sorry. This was a mistake. You're very…attractive but I can't do this."

"What's wrong?" she asked. "You don't like me?"

"You're stunning," Owen tried to avoid looking at her. "But I'm very drunk and I would never have done this if I was sober… I want to go back to my hotel."

"You want to talk and cuddle instead?' Celeste asked hopefully. She was obviously used to some of her clientele not rising to the occasion.

"No, thanks, I'll go back downstairs and wait for my friend." And for some weird reason, he shook her hand as he left. *Fuck!* What was wrong with him? 120 euros! What was he thinking? He wasn't a player! He should have known that he didn't have the guts to have sex with Celeste, with any prostitute! Why did he listen to Huw? And where was Huw? Was he OK? Owen imagined his friend being whipped ferociously, his balls trapped in a vice, pinioned by the frightening Ebony.

Owen shuffled back to the counter towards the madam with his tail between his legs.

"Finished?' The madam looked at him in mild surprise. "Yes, thank you. I'll wait for my friend if that's OK."

"He has another ten minutes," the madam said, more softly this time as she took in Owen's pale face. Those ten minutes dragged by painfully slowly as Owen tried to concentrate on an old *Playboy* magazine printed in Dutch and avoid eye contact with the madam.

At last Huw came clattering down the stairs, smiling broadly.

"Can we go now please?' Owen sighed. He just wanted to go to bed and forget about this sordid interlude.

"Yes, yes." Huw was blasé as they left the building. "How did it go then, Owen? Was Celeste any good? Did you come or what?"

As they passed the third window, Owen noticed that Celeste was back in her window seat in her underwear, ready for the next punter. He smiled wanly at her as they passed. She smiled back at him.

"I didn't do anything."

"What?" Huw stumbled over an old beer can as the walked towards the Botel.

"It just didn't feel right."

"That was a right waste of 120 euros, then…" Huw scoffed. "Well, I had a great time. That Ebony, wow, she was a hell of a girl. I had three orgasms in an hour! Amazing! She had legs like a ballerina and breasts like—"

"Shut it, OK! I don't want to hear about it!"

Huw wasn't listening. "Before we started, the madam made me wait for a bit in a jacuzzi in my undies with some other dudes. That was a bit weird. I put my nose under the water so I could feel the bubbles on my face but then I remembered a lot of other guys' balls had been in that water too, so I lifted my head after that."

Huw was still very pissed and almost fell over when he and Owen finally reached the Botel. "Get in and shut it will you! You'll wake everybody up."

"You're way too Puritan...i...cal, Owen, bach," Huw murmured sleepily. "We're in Europe now, not Ely!"

"It's not that different," Owen said under his breath as he heard Huw starting to snore. He watched the city's multi-coloured lights winking at him through the hotel window as he slowly fell into a deep sleep.

"Fuck, fuck, fuck!" Huw shouted, running into Owen's room in his underpants, two weeks after their return from Amsterdam. "Look! What on earth are these things?" He was holding his underpants away from his pubes and pushing his crotch towards Owen's face.

"Ugh, Huw man! I've just had my supper!" Owen pushed him away in disgust.

"Look at my pubes! There's something in there!

Something that's alive. It's moving, look, and it itches like the devil!"

"Well, Heff… It looks like you've got a dose of crabs!"

"What? How?" Huw's face was as pale as marble.

"Ebony?" Owen suggested, a smile lifting the corners of his mouth.

"Oh shit!" Huw sighed as he scratched at his pubic hair like a monkey. "What shall I do?"

"Go to the doctor and ask him for some ointment or something. That'll get rid of them easily enough. You did use a condom, I hope? You don't want anything worse than a dose of the crabs, do you…"

"Well, I don't remember, do I? I think I did, but I was pissed."

"Remember, you were in that jacuzzi with all those men, too!"

"Oh my God, oh my god!" Huw shouted in a panic. "I'm going to have a shower in some Dettol and then go to the doctor." He ran back into the bathroom like a whirlwind.

"Look at it like this! You came home with a free souvenir!"

Owen laughed as he settled down to watch *Big Brother*. He wasn't that worried about Huw – all those places insisted on their girls using protection, but this was the last time Huw would experiment with professional girls. They'd focus their attention on ordinary Welsh girls from now on!

Chapter 8

Mari

Mr Toyboy, 2008

"He's only 24 Mari…" Sara sighed, they were sharing a bottle of wine and watching a dvd in the flat.

"Yes, yes, I know that, but I can't stop thinking about him!"

"And he works for you!"

"And the prize for stating the bleeding obvious goes to…"

"I just don't want to see you fucking up again, that's all." Sara drained her wine at a gulp. "Never shit on your own doorstep… And he's your trainee for God's sake!"

"It's not as if I'm really old, you know," Mari said in her own defence. "It's only a nine year age gap. Look at Madonna and Guy Ritchie, Richard and Judy – there's 10 years between them and they're happy. And Joan Collins and Babs Windsor are 40 years older than their husbands!"

"Ugh!" Sara wrinkled her nose in disgust. "Imagine

being in bed with a young guy riding you and you having to stop to put more lube on and to hoist up your old saggy boobs from your belly!"

"Sara, you're disgusting! I'm 33 not 63! And he fancies me!"

"And why do you think that, Mrs Robinson?"

"I'm no Mrs Robinson. I'm too chicken to ask him out even!"

"I always thought you and Owen would end up together…"

"Owen's nice, but we're mates more than anything and he wasn't interested, if you remember. He likes blondes, anyway – air-heads. And he's had plenty of chances to ask me out."

"Well, if you really like this Jack guy, go for it. But be careful and don't make a tit of yourself. You know how gossip spreads in an office. You don't want to be the topic of conversation over the water cooler!"

"We haven't got a water cooler." Mari smirked.

"You know what I mean!" Sara wagged her finger at Mari.

Mari nodded. She knew only too well what people would say if Jack rebuffed her clumsy advances. And this was what had stopped her from asking him out. But to be honest, the URST (unresolved sexual tension, as the cool kids had it) she felt as she took sneaky looks at him as he worked at the desk opposite her, was too exciting to threaten with the harsh reality that she might be kidding herself.

She'd fancied Jack from day one. He was just her type. Tall, about 6 feet three, muscly, dark…perfect! He'd come to work with Celt TV on a media training course. When the boss originally told her she'd have to train this newbie, Mari was unimpressed as she imagined any trainee would be a spotty, know-it-all youth. The boss wanted them to work closely together and to produce as many TV ideas as possible for development for the next commissioning round. Mari had just secured a six part series on the history of different villages or towns called Bethlehem – not only in Wales but across the world, which would be a nice Christmas stocking filler and had garnered her quite a lot of kudos from her bosses.

Now, of course, she was delighted to be working closely with Jack. He was different to the other youngsters she'd met. He didn't swagger or brag even though he had a first class honours degree in Film Studies. He was really artistic and could draw brilliantly and had a fantastically dry sense of humour. He also had a really cute face, a sexy body and no baggage (kids or ex-es). The only fly in the ointment was his youth and her age… But did that really matter? They'd settled into a routine of flirting via email – they would make up playful little poems about each other. Mari hadn't behaved like this since she was a lovestruck teen. She tried to keep the relationship professional and up 'til now, they hadn't been out socially at all. But tomorrow night, she might have a chance to take things further as they were all going on an office away day. The bosses would force these away days on them every six months or so to encourage "team bonding".

They were going on a trip on an old steamboat, the *Waverley*, sailing from Penarth to Weston Super Mare and back and then having a meal in a posh restaurant in the Marina. Quite a pointless exercise in Mari's opinion: sailing somewhere, not disembarking and then sailing back again. Thank the Lord, there was a bar on the boat according to the website. Without that it would be intolerable, a real *Voyage of the Damned*. Of course, another big plus point for the trip was the potential for a good flirt with Jack. He'd teased her about the trip in an email: "Fancy playing a bit of *Titanic* with me on the *Waverley* tomorrow?"

"Yes indeed," Mari had replied. "Bring your pencils and your sketchbooks and I might model for you. But I don't have a locket…" *Shit!* Was she being too forward referencing the famous scene in the movie in which Di Caprio sketched a portrait of a naked Kate Winslet? She could sense herself blushing as she watched him read her email. But she could see he liked the message as broke into a cheeky smile. A few seconds later, his reply pinged into her inbox: "OK. I'll make sure my pencil's sharp!" Oh God, this flirtation was like something out of a *Carry On…* film! She smiled at him and then pretended to resume typing.

He had to fancy her, didn't he? He might just be using her to help him progress with his media career… No, he didn't seem the over ambitious type. He had told Mari that he wasn't even sure if he wanted to pursue a long-time career in the media as he wasn't keen on the bulk of this particular job, which was about appealing to fickle and boorish TV commissioners. They didn't want innovation, they wanted the mainstream big idea – the new *X Factor* or *Strictly….*

Mari was focused on looking her best on the *Waverley* day trip and was still deliberating what she should wear half an hour before she had to leave the house She asked Sara, "What should I wear? This floral dress – slightly frumpy yet sophisticated? Or a t-shirt and mini-skirt – playful but immature?"

"What about frumpy and immature – could be the perfect combo?" Sara chortled as she referenced one of their favourite TV comedies, *Spaced.*

Mari had huffed, throwing clothes about in frustration. "You're not helping Sara!" *Great, she'd torn her new pair of tights as well!*

"Wear the floral dress. You don't want to look like mutton in that mini skirt."

"You're sure?" Mari hadn't been at all sure about the dress.

"Yes! You don't want to come on too strong. And it is a work do."

"OK, OK! I'm late as it is!" Mari had rushed back to her bedroom to complete her toilette.

To Mari's surprise, the boat trip was turning out to be quite pleasant. Everyone, including their two elderly bosses, was in a good mood and determined to enjoy the bar's charms. And after spending an hour on the waves and a few glasses of wine, the atmosphere was cheery and light. Jack sat at her side, looking extremely sexy in his jeans and black shirt. He'd cut his hair and looked younger than ever. She couldn't help fancying the pants off him. Was she a pervert? What did it matter, she thought to herself. She was still young and quite attractive – she had to take a chance sometime. And now her perfect opportunity to take things further with Jack had arrived. But bloody Owen was walking towards them – what did he want now? Mmm, he looked quite cute today, too, in his grey shirt, she thought tipsily.

"Jack, Harriet wants to talk to you." Owen smiled at him pleasantly.

"What does she want now?"

"I think she wants to check your menu choices for the meal later."

"Watch it, or she'll trap you in a tortuous conversation about her bloody kids!" Mari knew that Jack wouldn't waste his time prattling with Harriet, the office bore. She was one of those mumzillas who thought that everyone else was as interested in her kids' activities as she was. Owen and Mari had shared several jokes about Harriet and her obsession with her kids, hoping the two girls would grow up to be crack-addicts or prostitutes, just so they could see Harriet's face when she realised.

Owen sat down and handed Mari a glass of booze. "G and T, Mari?"

"Thanks Owen, just the thing." Owen was thoughtful, fair play to him.

"So how are you enjoying this trip then?"

"It's much better than I thought it would be." Mari smiled as she looked over at Jack, who was obviously trying to escape Harriet's clutches.

"Thank God there's a bar eh? Well, Mari, we haven't had a chat for a while... How's your love life these days?"

"What?" Mari asked in surprise. *Shit!* He must have noticed her checking Jack out. If Owen knew, then everyone in the office knew: her friend wasn't known for being the first with the office gossip as he tended to live in his own world and not listen to idle chit chat.

"Well, I wanted to ask you something... I've been meaning to ask you for a while now..."

"I know what you're going to say, Owen." She might as well come out with the truth as obviously everyone must already know her secret.

"Do you?"

"Jack's too young for me and I work with him – blah, blah. I know all this but I *really* like him…" That was it! It was out! The bloody gin was to blame, she'd have never said it if she hadn't had three doubles…

Owen said quietly, "I thought so… But don't you think he's too young for you? And what do you have in common apart from work?"

Bloody Owen! He thought she was too old for Jack, just because he hadn't fancied her, it didn't mean that Jack wouldn't – did it?

"A lot, thanks Owen. He's really mature for his age, a lot more mature than most guys I know who are quite a bit older than him. He's bright too," she looked at him pointedly.

"So you're telling me that you fancy young Jack because of his brains?" Owen rolled his eyes.

"Yes, because at least he knows how to use them!" Mari barked. "It's none of your business anyway. I'm going now, Owen, before we fall out!" She got up and walked towards Jack without giving Owen a backward glance. She didn't want to fall out with Owen, he was an OK bloke, a friend. Perhaps he was trying to help, but she didn't want him ruining her plans with Jack.

"Hi Harriet. I'm just going to steal Jack for a minute. I need a light." Mari grabbed Jack's hand as she pulled him away from Harriet.

215

"Thank God!" Jack sighed. "It was like being stuck in a spider's web. And she didn't want to talk about the menu at all. Bloody Owen!'"

"Yeah, I think Owen was winding you up. Anyway, come over here so we can have a private chat." The gins had given Mari Dutch courage and she knew she had to speak to Jack now about her feelings, in case Owen beat her to it and ruined everything.

"So, Jack, are you enjoying yourself?" she asked as she lit his cigarette for him. He was obviously flirting with her at this point as he cupped her hand as she flicked the lighter; his eyes looking at her intently. Oh my God, even his touch made her want to swoon!

"Yes, now I'm with you," he smiled at her warmly.

"If you're trying to get out of writing that treatment about the brass band in the valleys, you can think again, mister!" Mari laughed and patted his arm. *Ooh... His muscles felt so hard and strong...*

"No, I'm not! Just saying that I'm enjoying your company, that's all."

"Thanks... I like your company too..." Mari looked into his beautiful green eyes. God, he was gorgeous! And because she was a teensy bit drunk, it felt perfectly natural to lean towards him and kiss him. The kiss was lovely and Mari felt a huge wave of lust wash over her. After several seconds, she broke the kiss unwillingly and whispered in his ear, "We have to be careful, in case we're seen." Their colleagues were ambling along the deck, most as drunk as skunks by now, but they might still spot her and Jack canoodling. She had to be discreet. And she didn't want them laughing and pulling her leg – it could put Jack off.

"What, are you ashamed of me?" Jack asked, a flash of disappointment in his eyes. Mari gripped his hand.

"Not at all, Jack. I've fancied you for ages… But I don't want them laughing at us because I'm older than you… Or thinking that I'm taking advantage, 'cause I'm your boss, in a way…"

"I know, it's sexy, isn't it? But you're only a bit older than me… And you're lovely…" Jack smiled at her mischievously and kissed her again. Mari threw her arms around his neck and kissed him back. Her day couldn't have turned out better.…

"But what about when you get back to work?" Sara asked when Mari told her the story the next day.

Mari had spent the night with Jack and his stamina and ability in the bedroom had completely bewitched her. "We're going to be completely professional, of course," Mari said briskly, although she expected they'd be sending each other dirty emails whilst pretending to work. "We're both grown-ups, we're single and we can do what we like. I'm not really his boss, you know. Can't you be happy for us?"

"Of course I'm happy for you, you silly moo! He seems to be making you happy, so far… And if it's good enough for Richard and Judy…"

"Exactly!" Mari laughed and she left for work on the Monday with wings on her stilettos.

Over the next few months, she and Jack grew closer. Everyone at Celt knew about the relationship and apart from some snippy comments from Owen, no one had said anything derogatory. Mari made sure that they behaved completely professionally in the office and Jack respected that. She didn't want anyone saying they were unprofessional and taking the piss. She'd met a few of Jack's friends and they were a good bunch – although a bit wild at times. Well, they were only in their early twenties. In the beginning, Mari enjoyed going to gigs, downing shots and staying up late smoking spliffs with Jack and his flatmates, Trig and Sherlock. But one night a couple of months into their relationship, she realised the age gap might become problematic when Jack tried to persuade her to come out to yet another gig (the third that week).

"Come on, Mari. You'll really like this band, they're like Nirvana but even cooler…"

"Cooler than Nirvana? No way!" Mari laughed as she put her feet up on the sofa.

"Come on Grandma!" Jack teased her. "You're showing your age now!" Mari realised that the nine year age gap was a whole generation gap…well, half maybe. Whilst she'd been listening to Nirvana at uni, Jack had still been in nappies – almost. She started to feel uncomfortable. Although she didn't want kids yet, the old clock was ticking. She was 33, she didn't want to wait too long in case her eggs went off. And she didn't want people mistaking her for her child's grandmother! But she didn't want to finish with Jack either. It would be better to slow things down perhaps, before she really fell for him. The age gap would never change and would get more obvious as she got older.

She kissed Jack lightly on the lips and said sweetly, "You go tonight. I'm going to watch dvds with Sara. I haven't got the stamina to go out every night."

"You've got plenty of stamina my girl!" Jack leered. "More than enough actually."

Mari turned to face him, "Listen, Jack. I really like our arrangement but I don't want anything too serious OK? I know you don't want to be too serious either. You're only young and this is a bit of fun. We get along really well and the sex is great. But I'll want to settle down soon…"

"You're finishing with me?" Jack stared at her.

"No, I still want to see you. But I don't want anything serious…because of the age gap… I don't want to hold you back…"

"So…sex and no strings?" Jack asked, his face brightening.

"Exactly!" Mari nodded. "And if we find someone who's the same age as us who wants a serious relationship, then we can go back to being just good friends."

"You're amazing, Mari!" Jack smiled at her, not believing his luck. "The best of both worlds!"

"I'm so pleased you understand." Mari was relieved. Thank God, Jack understood her. But they were always on the same wavelength… "Have we got some time before you go out?" Mari dared to grab his crotch. She was turning into Samantha from *Sex and the City* (well, apart from the designer clothes, the Rolex and the Botox!).

"Are you sure you've got enough energy?" Jack teased.

"More than enough!" Mari laughed as she dragged him into the bedroom.

As Mari revelled in yet another steamy sex session with Jack, she smiled to herself. She was an independent woman who knew what she wanted in life and for once, she was getting it.

Owen

Miss-take, 2008

"Well, if this guy is on a training course, he'll sling his hook in a few months anyway won't he?" Huw asked Owen as his flatmate complained yet again about the cuckoo in the Celt nest.

"Usually a trainee would move on, yes," Owen puffed. "But because he's so frickin' brilliant, the bosses have offered him a researcher contract already! Almost on my level and I'm 34! He's 10 years younger than me – the bloody smug embryo!

"They all think he's the next Spielberg in the office. Even Mari gets on really well with him…"

"Aha!" Huw said. "Now we're getting to the nub of the issue. Is jealously rearing its little green snout here?"

"Well, she's always 'too busy' to go out for a pint after work with me these days… But funnily enough she's never too busy to go for a drink with Jack! And they have all these little 'in-jokes' at work. I'm surprised he's performing so well at his job considering the amount of time he spends making cow eyes at Mari and flirting with her every whip stitch." Owen shook his head and opened a can of San Miguel. It was hard for him to ignore the burgeoning chemistry between Mari and Jack as he was sat at the same block of desks at them. He was sick of the giggles and overt emailing; why wasn't she still interested in him? She used to email him a funny joke or internet link to look at; but these days, they barely spoke outside work and he really missed her company. Fuck!

"I thought you weren't interested in Mari anyway. You knocked her back after that snog in Boom Box…" Huw reminded him.

Owen turned to his friend, "I think I've made a big

mistake mate… I think Mari might be the one… I can't stop thinking about her…"

"Well, you can always try a bit of sabotage," Huw said, scratching his head.

"What? Setting Jack up in work? Nah, I can't. I'm not sly or clever enough to do that and if Mari found out, well, I could kiss any chance with her goodbye."

"Mmm, yeah. But there might be another way? A pretty young thing in the office, perhaps? Someone you could set him up with on a blind date so he forgets about Mari?"

"No, Mari's the only youngish single woman there – the rest are too old or too married."

"You've only got one option left then."

"What's that then?"

"You'll have to make the first move before him. Survival of the fittest, my shy friend. And to be honest, you should have done this ages ago, before this Jack came on the scene."

"I know, but I always thought in the back of my mind that Mari and I would end up together, sometime. When the time was right."

"This isn't *When Harry Met Sally*, Owen," Huw said impatiently. "'He Who Dares Wins'… You're way too fatalistic leaving these things to chance! It's no wonder you're always picking crap women. Now, when are you going to ask Mari out?"

"Well, we've got that work away day thing tomorrow," Owen said hopefully. "Some team-bonding bollocks that the boss insists we go on… Might be a chance there."

"Is alcohol a part of this day trip?"

"I should bloody hope so. We're going on a steamer ship from Penarth to Weston and back."

"Ah, a ship… A perfect opportunity for romance – a real life *Loveboat*, unless you vomit everywhere again!" Huw chortled.

"Nah, I don't get seasick. But I hope that Jack is as sick as a dog!"

"Well, you'll have to prepare yourself. Perhaps Jack is planning to make his move as well!"

The next morning, Owen dressed carefully and showed his sartorial choices to Huw. A new grey Diesel shirt, dark blue Levis and black Converse trainers. Classic, yet not overly smart for a social occasion, he hoped. Mari always dressed well and he knew she'd be checking out his looks – he remembered how she'd teased him when he'd tried to grow a goatee last year. And, of course, bloody Jack always looked like a Topman mannequin.

"Which jacket did you have in mind?" Huw asked, Sergeant Major-like.

"The khaki one?"

"Ugh! No! What do you think you'll be doing? Recreating *Apocalypse Now*? Wear your leather jacket, it

223

makes you look reasonably cool even though you're a nerd. And it might be cold on that bloody boat."

"OK, Gran!" Owen fetched his leather jacket obediently.

"Remember to sit next to her as soon as you can and don't let Jack near her!" Huw warned. "And watch out for icebergs!"

Well, this was a pointless bloody journey, Owen thought miserably as he sat shivering on the ancient steamship. He'd already failed to secure a seat next to Mari. That bloody Jack, like a sly snake, had succeeded in planting his greedy buttocks next to her as soon as they'd got on the boat. Owen was stuck next to Harriet, the office bore; Harriet only wanted to talk about two things, her daughters – 11 and nine years old respectively. Stephanie this, Chloe that. Perfectly normal children, but miraculous creations in their obsessive mother's eyes.

"Oh my God, Owen, Chloe is so clever, she frightens me sometimes," Harriet enthused as a glum Owen drank his lager beside her.

"Mm?" Owen wasn't even faking an interest in her boring chatter. The woman was so thick-skinned, he doubted she'd notice if he fell into a coma beside her.

"Yes, well, I was telling her we were going on the *Waverley* steam ship and the little one knew everything about the ship's history! Just like that! Clive and I were shocked!"

Clive was Harriet's unfortunate husband and even though Owen had never met him, he felt he knew him all too well. He knew for example that Clive must be a complete twat to have married a monster like Harriet.

"And Stephanie, well, she's done so well in her gymnastics tournament that she has to suffer a lot of jealousy from the other girls. But I told her, 'Stephy, in this world you have winners and losers. Make sure you're a winner.' And fair play to her, she hasn't lost a tournament yet. Do you want to see a photo of her with her trophies?"

"Sorry, Harriet, I need to go to the gents. I'll see you later," Owen got up quickly and heaved a sigh of relief. He looked around and saw Jack and Mari cosied up next to each other. She was laughing uproariously at one of the oaf's stupid jokes. Right, after his toilet pit-stop, he'd go over there and join them. He'd buy Mari a gin and tonic and wow her with some funny chat and hopefully Jack would get the message and fuck off.

As he approached them, he noticed how beautiful Mari looked today. She wore a pretty floral dress that suited her tall shape perfectly. Her green eyes were the exact same shade as the sea around them and the way her dark hair was blowing in the wind reminded him of Kate Winslet in *Titanic* (even though the film was shit, he had watched it as he was quite taken with Ms Winslet's charms). Why hadn't he asked Mari out last year? How could he compete with Handsome Jack? The bloke had everything! Gift of the gab, brains, looks, physique… He had to get rid of him somehow. Suddenly, he had a brainwave.

"Oh, hi Jack, Harriet wants to speak to you,' he said as he approached the couple on his way back from the loos.

"Shit! What does she want now?" Jack said, impatiently. And off he went! Owen smiled to himself. Now for the charm offensive. He didn't have much time – he'd have to work fast before the boy wonder reappeared. He gave Mari the G and T (which went down well) and then, bang, straight in there (thanks to the lagers he'd consumed) but of course, she had the wrong end of the stick. Why was his love life so complicated? Why couldn't he just get the right girl for once?

"I wanted to ask you something… something I've been meaning to ask you for a while…"

"I know what you're going to say, Owen."

Oh my God, did she know that he loved her? Of course, she had to realise the attraction was still there between them.

"That Jack's too young for me and I work with him. I know that but I really like him…"

226

Owen's heart sank to his shoes and he tried to pretend that he'd known her secret all along.

He had to talk her out of this! Surely she wasn't serious about this stupid kid? He looked at her face – she was deadly serious! And then she got up and walked away. Great, he was too late and the only thing he'd succeeded in doing was to upset her and make the boy wonder even more appealing. *Shit, shit shit!* He'd lost his chance. He might as well forget about Mari and any future they might have had together. He looked at his watch and realised they had another hour and a half to go on this wretched boat. He drained his pint and walked slowly towards the bar.

Just as Owen thought his day couldn't get any worse, the final nail in the coffin was delivered. He spotted Mari and Jack snogging – enthusiastically – not quite out of sight of the rest of the party. He turned on his heel in disgust and waited his turn at the bar. Who was there, but Harriet.

"Owen, Owen, the man himself! Come here so I can show you a piccy of Stephy!" Harriet said happily as she burrowed in her wallet tipsily.

"Harriet, I don't want to hear or see anything about your kids, OK? There's nothing worse than listening to a boring mother go on and on about her boring kids. They're nothing special OK! They're normal! And that's fine! So if you don't mind, I just want to get a drink and be on my own." He grabbed his pint from the barman and left Harriet open mouthed at the bar. "Bloody boats… *Loveboat*, my arse!" He muttered to himself as he went stumbling towards the stern.

"Oh dear," he heard. He looked up and saw a pretty girl standing there. "You look like you need a shot of something cheerful," she said as she sat beside him. "Have this." Owen smiled at her and accepted the shot gratefully.

"I'm Lucy," she said confidently.

"Owen."

"Owen, my favourite name." She smiled downing her shot in one. "I'm with a hen party – it's a frickin nightmare! Half the girls are spewing over the side and the other half have gone off with some trolls!"

"I'm here with work. It's shit." Owen looked at her and noted her pretty dark curls and warm brown eyes. Much prettier than Mari's stinking green cat's eyes.

"Thank God, I found you, Owen," Lucy said happily as she put her arm around his shoulder.

Owen smiled back. "Thank God!"

Three months later and brown-eyed Lucy was a permanent fixture in the flat. Huw was not amused.

"Mate, she's a control-freak," Huw said, blunt as ever, as he and Owen rushed around the flat, trying to tidy up before their guests arrived for supper. Lucy wanted to meet Owen's friends, so he'd reluctantly invited Mari and Jack and Huw and Elin (who was by now Huw's official girlfriend and not just a convenient arrangement) for a meal. Thanks to Marks and Sparks, compiling the menu was easy enough, although he had to ensure Lucy's meal was gluten free and veggie friendly of course.

"She has high standards, that's all."

"High standards? You had shit from her because you didn't let her pick out *our* new bread bin! Before long, she'll be choosing your pants for you as well!" Huw nagged, not realising that Owen was blushing as Lucy had selected most of his outfits recently, even his underwear.

"You could make much more of yourself Owen," she'd told him as he deliberated over buying an expensive Ted Baker shirt in Howells. "You're not a student any more; you should dress like a man about town – 'dress to impress' – then you might get that promotion!"

She had a point. But she could be a control freak as well. Last week, she'd hidden his razor because she wanted to see more stubble on his cheeks. But she just wanted him to be the best he could and there was nothing wrong with that was there? Of course, he hadn't told Huw about the razor business…

"Listen, Huw, I know you're not a big fan of Lucy's. But try and get on with her will you? She really likes you.

"Bollocks." Huw puffed. "She pretends to be nice to

me when you're around but I know her little game… She wants me out so she can move in!"

"You're talking nonsense now Huw." Owen chuckled, although he did have a kernel of doubt in his stomach; there might be some truth to Huw's suspicions. Before Huw could comment further, the doorbell rang and who was there but Lucy herself, along with an awkward looking Mari and Jack.

Over compensating, Owen greeted them effusively, "Oh great guys, you're here. Dinner will be ready soon… Come in and I'll get you all a drink…"

Lucy had already pushed her way in through the door. Owen clocked Mari giving her an irritated look. Shit! He hoped the evening wouldn't be a complete wash-out. "I'll open some wine," Lucy trilled as she walked confidently into the kitchen; demonstrating that she knew her way around Owen's flat.

Huw and Elin were already sitting in the lounge drinking their cans of lager. "Huw, Elin, you know Mari… And here's Jack."

"Great to meet you, bro," Jack shook Huw's hand with gusto.

Huw raised a subtle eyebrow at Owen when Jack used the term "bro". Owen nodded – he was glad that Huw could see that Jack was a complete dickhead.

It was apparent from the start that Lucy and Mari wouldn't be best friends either.

From the moment Lucy opened her mouth, Owen could see Mari bridle. "Mari, I love your dress," Lucy said. "Last year's Primark is it?"

Mari shook her head and said, "No, this year's Topshop…"

"Really?" Lucy said. "I could have sworn… Well, I don't go to Primark very often, of course, in case the boss sees me!"

Lucy worked in the expensive Karen Millen store as she kept mentioning in conversation. "Karen Millen is the best, Mari, if you want something classy… Of course it's quite expensive…"

"And a bit old fashioned," Mari added with a malicious smile, she knew very well that Lucy was wearing a Millen outfit.

"Horses for courses," Owen said hurriedly, before a catfight broke out. "Now I think dinner's ready, if you would all move to the table, please."

"Oh you're so cute tonight, Owen." Lucy patted his cheek as they moved to the table. "Playing host… I think it's adorable!"

Owen cringed, he could see Huw smirking at Mari. Why did Lucy talk to him as if he was a five-year-old? Fuck's sake! He wanted everyone, well, Mari in particular to think he wore the trousers in this relationship!

"This steak is very tasty, Owen," Jack said politely as he tried to cut his steak unsuccessfully.

"It looks a bit well done to me," Lucy laughed. "Owen hasn't got much of a clue in the kitchen."

Owen could see Mari rolling her eyes at Huw and his friend lifting his eyebrows back at Mari. What was wrong with them both? Lucy wasn't that bad! At least she was old enough to get into the clubs in town, unlike baby Jack! Owen wouldn't admit this to anyone, not even Huw, but seeing Mari there tonight, so pretty and happy, with Jack at her side, was a real kick in the guts. Lucy, with all her faults was better than nothing, he thought bitterly. After all, he was in his mid-thirties now and it was slim pickings out there. He was startled out of his reverie as he heard Lucy say: "Of course, when we move in together, I'll look after the cuisine side of things!" She laughed, stroking Owen's arm territorially. "Owen can focus on filling the dishwasher!"

Moving in? Owen panicked as he visualised these words flashing in neon above him. He was desperate for someone to share his life, but not that desperate! He could see only too clearly how their lives together would be – their home would be a Habitat cemetery and he would be buried alive like a mummy in designer clothing amongst the carefully chosen soft furnishings.

Thank God, Huw jumped to the rescue: "Moving in? You've only been together for five minutes!"

"Long enough to know that we suit each other perfectly!" Lucy beamed at Owen, her smile only slightly fixed. But Owen couldn't say a word – he kept trying to cut his steak as if his life depended on it and in his frenzy, he managed to tip a whole glass of red wine over Lucy's new white dress. "Owen!" Lucy screamed as her dress turned pink thanks to the cheap plonk.

"Sorry, Lucy," Owen tried to mop up the mess with his serviette.

"You need some white wine on that, Lucy,' Mari said throwing a full glass of white wine over Lucy's lap. Lucy shrieked and ran into the bathroom. By now, everyone had abandoned their main course and the atmosphere was terrible.

"Do you think we should go, Owen?" Jack asked quietly.

"Yes, Lucy is very upset." Mari was puffing with laughter.

"Listen, I've had enough of you and Huw taking the piss out of Lucy tonight. I was looking forward to you all getting to know her better and look what you've done!"

"Us?" Huw asked. "We didn't throw red wine all over her Owen!"

"Owen, she's awful," Mari whispered. "She's got you under her thumb and things will get even worse if you let her move in with you!"

"Yes, and you kept that little development quiet – where am I supposed to go if she moves in?" Huw whinged.

"She's not moving in, OK!" Owen shouted.

"What did you say? Lucy stood there in her sopping wet, pale pink frock, her eyes burning with fury.

"We'd better go," Elin whispered loudly to Huw.

"Yes, erm… Thanks very much for supper," Jack said politely as he grabbed Mari's arm.

"See you tomorrow mate, I'll stay over with Elin tonight." Huw led the stampede out of the flat.

"Well, thanks a lot, Owen," Lucy spat at him, "for ruining the evening! You know very well that I'm serious about our relationship and here you are telling all and sundry that you don't give a shit!"

"I didn't say that," Owen said. "It's just early days that's all and way too soon to talk about moving in together."

"When are you going to grow up Owen? You're pushing forty for fuck's sake! It's time for you and Huw to stop behaving like students! You're pathetic!"

Owen could finally see her true character for the first time and realised that he actually disliked her. Huw was right, she was a control freak and he was six whole years away from being 40, the cheeky cow. His life would be hell if he moved in with her. He'd better end it now before she became even more clingy and demanding.

"Lucy, I'm really sorry, but I think we want different things and we better finish it before you get hurt."

"Oh, no, Owen Davies. Don't you dare finish with me!" Lucy eyed him with pure malice.

"Well, I'm sorry, but I reckon that's the best thing for both of us," Owen said quietly.

"Better for you, you mean. But I refuse."

"What?" Owen couldn't believe his ears. The mad bint wouldn't let him finish with her? What the hell was this? "I know it's hard for you to hear this Lucy. But we don't want the same things. There's no point carrying on with this, it's not going anywhere."

"You'll thank me in the end," Lucy told him, with a strange smile on her face. "Now, come and help me wash up and clear this mess…"

Owen stared at her as she carried the dirty plates into the kitchen. How the hell would he get rid of her now?

He avoided the incessant phone calls and numerous texts for a few days after the dinner party, hoping she'd get the message. But one evening, a week or so later, it was obvious that she hadn't. He'd just come back from work and let himself into the flat. It had been another shitty day watching Mari and Jack flirt with each other like horny adolescents and he just wanted to watch some crap TV and drink a beer in peace. He walked into the sitting room and to his horror, Lucy was sitting there on the sofa bold as brass. There was no sign of Huw; shit, had she killed him or something?

"Owen," she jumped up enthusiastically and kissed him. He tried to pull away but she had a vice like grip around his neck. Fuck! Hadn't she got the message last week? He managed to pull her arms away. "Lucy, what are you doing here? I thought I'd made myself clear last Friday. We're finished. I don't want to see you anymore. And I need the spare key back; you can't just come in here when you want. It's over."

She laughed, "Oh, you're not still holding a grudge over that little tiff are you? Come on Owen, you're worse than a woman!"

She leaned in again to kiss him and Owen moved away from her quickly.

"I'm serious Lucy, I don't want to go out with you any more."

"Oh, you're just punishing me because I slagged off your cooking the other night! I was only joking babe; you're so sensitive. Now, get the glasses, I've got a bottle of red in my bag." Lucy brandished the bottle of wine at him.

"No, I've just come back from work and I've got nothing more to say. I'm really sorry if I've hurt you in any way but we've both got to move on. And it's really out of order and highly creepy, to be honest, that you just let yourself in to the flat without my permission…" He was trying hard not to lose it with her as she was obviously as mad as a basket of frogs and shouting at her might tip her over the edge; well, if she wasn't over the edge already.

"You don't mean that Owen," Lucy said calmly. "You're pushing me away because you're scared of commitment. I know you love me…"

He'd never told her that he loved her; she was scaring him now. She was obviously in deep denial. Shit! She could go all *Fatal Attraction* on him any minute if he didn't play it cool. If she wouldn't leave; he would have to, it was the only way to get rid of her.

"Listen, erm… I'm actually on my way out; I've got a work thing on… So I can't stay and talk… You'll have to go…"

"I'll come with you, I've always wanted to meet some more of your work buddies. I could drop a few hints with those bosses of yours that they should give you a pay rise!" Lucy chortled and Owen felt a chilling fear. Nothing was getting through to her.

"No, you can't come, Lucy. I'm sorry, but we're finished and please leave the house key when you go." With that, he turned on his heels and literally ran out of the flat. Fuck! He'd have to change the locks and everything. He had a full blown stalker on his hands!

The next couple of weeks were pure hell. He decided to ask Mari for some advice as he was at his wits end. He'd changed the locks and had also changed his routine, such as waiting until Huw had given the all clear before he went home to the flat, in case she'd turned up on his doorstep again. Huw had tried to tell her to sling her hook the second time she came round, but it had fallen on deaf ears.

Mari listened intently as he shared the sorry tale with her over a much needed pint after work.

"Oh my God, Owen, you must have had a fit when you saw her on the sofa! It's like that scene at the end of *Rosemary's Baby* ..."

"But even scarier!" Owen nodded morosely.

"Have you contacted the police?"

"Don't you think that's a bit extreme?"

"She did enter your flat without permission..."

"But I'd given her the key..."

"Mmm...bad move! What does Huw think?"

"Well, apart from suggesting throwing a bucket of water over her head when she comes round again, not much."

"I think you should call the cops, just in case she turns violent... To be honest with you, I didn't like her as soon as I saw her; so pushy and controlling..."

"She hid my razor once, cos she wanted me to grow a stubble," Owen said, glad to get all Lucy's craziness off his chest.

"No! Oh my God!" Mari was riveted and she lit a cigarette. There was a silver lining to this mess with Lucy; at least he was getting to spend some quality time with Mari because of this "crisis."

"And she insisted that I only wear Calvin Klein boxer shorts… She threw my other ones away."

"Frickin hell! No, deffo call the police; a man's boxer shorts are his own private kingdom!" Mari said faking solemnity, and quoting a line from *Blackadder 2*. Owen laughed getting the reference immediately. It was a ridiculous situation to be in – but at least with Mari he could have a good laugh about it. God, she was so pretty and funny; why hadn't he pursued her further on the *Waverley* instead of giving up and pulling bloody psycho Lucy? He wondered how serious she was about Jack and decided to do a bit of fishing.

"Enough about my dramas; how are things with you and young Jack?" Hah! "Young Jack" would hopefully pass on the subliminal message to Mari that this toyboy was way too young for her.

"Oh, he's great fun," said Mari. "We have a good laugh, he lets me have my freedom; he's certainly not a crazy stalker, thank God."

"Oh, that's good," *Shit!* She sounded as if she was really happy with him. Bugger!

"Any issues with the age gap?"

"Well, he'd never heard of *Twin Peaks* which was a tad worrying."

"Oh my God. Young people these days!"

"Yeah, and he likes to go out a lot more than me and never gets hangovers!"

"Yes, I'm a pipe and slippers man, these days," Owen nodded, hoping she'd realise that he was a much more suitable candidate for love.

"But then again," Mari brightened, "you and Lucy were the same age and look how that turned out!"

Owen felt even more depressed, now.

"Aw, it'll be OK, Owen, I'm sure Lucy'll get the message in the end," Mari patted his hand.

But Mari was wrong.

Huw and he spent most of their nights crouched on the sitting room floor hiding from Lucy and this was a full month after the dinner party!

"For God's sake, Owen," Huw said as they both knelt on the carpet like cowards as the doorbell rang incessantly. "You have to put a stop to this!"

"What do you suggest? I've told her face to face; I've written emails and texts; I've changed the locks, my phone number; what more can I do?"

"I think it's time to call in the big guns…"

"What, the police?"

"Well, yes," Huw said stolidly. "Lucy is obviously a stalker in the making and things could get nasty. I don't want to wake up one morning and find your body in bits in bin bags in the lounge!"

"Thanks for that cheery image!" Owen was starting to fear Huw was speaking the truth. After all, crimes of passion and a woman scorned were constant themes in the tabloids and Mari was adamant that he should get the fuzz involved. He rang the police the next day and awkwardly explained his dilemma. Fair play, they were very sympathetic. "Stalking is a serious matter, Mr Davies," the policeman said. "We'll call on Ms Jenkins and have a word with her."

Owen felt much happier and, apart from sending him a ghoulish funeral wreath with a card that read "RIP Owen and Lucy", he never saw or heard from her again.

"Next time, try and pick a normal woman will you!" Huw said wearily as he watched Owen toss the wreath into the bin.

"Like who?" Owen sighed.

"Well, what about Mari for example? You know she's the one for you! I see you giving that Jack the side eye when you think no-one is looking!"

"Mari seems perfectly happy with Jack, Huw, so there's no point thinking about that is there?" Owen sulked.

"Listen, mate," Huw said as he watched his friend slumped on the sofa about to watch a Radiohead concert on the TV. "It's just a matter of time and Mari will have had enough of Jack. He's a young buck in his twenties and she's in her thirties. He wants to go out with his mates and get pissed and she wants to settle down. It's a fling, you'll see."

"I don't believe that, Huw. They've been together for a while now and he's the whole package."

"Apart from one important element…maturity. No, these things never last. Don't you remember that Maggie Lewis?"

"Mari isn't like Maggie! She was much older than me!"

"Yes, but it's a similar scenario… A bit of patience and perseverance and you'll see that I'm right. OK, why don't you ask that Jack out for a pint so you can get some info about him and Mari? Find out how serious things really are between them. You've had her perspective, but you don't know what his intentions are…he's probably ready to move on to the next cougar…"

"You're not as dumb as you look." Owen's countenance brightened.

"Know your enemy. The first rule of warfare. And if you want to win, you need to find out more about Jack."

Jack agreed quite readily to a pint in the Cayo Arms after work later that week. Owen suggested that they drink their pints with chasers so he could get Jack tipsy enough to reveal juicy details about his relationship with Mari. So far the plan was going well as Jack supped his fourth pint happily.

"So Jack, how are things with you and Mari?" Owen asked, eyeing his prey like a hawk.

"Mari's really cool – she's not like other girls. She's a great sex-buddy!"

Was this the "yoof" jargon for lover?

"Sex-buddy?"

"Yeah, she doesn't want any strings 'cause I'm too young for her and she's too old for me. She'll want to have kids soon so she doesn't want to be serious with me… It's just sex really until she finds an older bloke she can be serious with," Jack said as he lit the wrong end of his cigarette.

"And she told you all this?"

"Yup." Jack dropped his cigarette on the floor. "The best of both worlds. Sex on tap but freedom to go off with other people."

"And Mari's happy with this arrangement?"

"Well, that's what she said. Another pint, mate?" Jack rose unsteadily to his feet.

"Yeah, pint of Fosters please, mate." Owen grinned. So, neither Mari or Jack were serious about each other then. There was hope. He smiled to himself as he lit his cigarette. This time, he'd succeed…

Chapter 9

Mari

Mr Perfect, 2007

Mari was busy typing an email to her boss, explaining a new idea she had about a documentary programme about Welsh UFOs when she clocked an email from Owen in her in-box. The subject heading read, "Invitation". She opened the email:

"Hi Mari
Are you free to go out for a quick drink with me tonight? I need to discuss something personal with you. Cayo Arms at 6?
Owen x"

Something personal? Was he thinking about quitting his job? She knew he was fed up with working on a dry history series and wanted to move from researching to producing. She turned to look at him but he was busy on the phone. Well, she was very fond of him and if he wanted advice, she was happy to listen. And Jack was going out with the boys tonight.

She replied to the email:

"Hi Owen. Intriguing! Looking forward to finding out more.

Mari x"

"Are you going somewhere tonight?" Jack asked as he watched her applying lipstick after they'd finished work.

"I'm going to the pub for a drink with Owen." She was so pleased the relationship with Jack was casual. She didn't care if he was going out with his mates tonight where he'd probably pull a young girl. He was like her little brother really – well, a little brother she knew "intimately". Uh oh! That sounded disgusting.

Owen walked up to her desk. "You ready?"

Jack laughed. "Watch this one, Mari. When I went out drinking with him, he got me really drunk!"

"It's not my fault that you're a lightweight." Owen laughed.

"I'll see you tomorrow then, Jack." Mari gave him a peck on the cheek in farewell and followed Owen out of the office.

"What do you fancy? G and T?" Owen asked, as they both stood at the bar in the Cayo Arms.

"Yes please." For the first time, Mari clocked his muscular arms. Gosh, Owen was quite buff. He must have been working out recently, because the last time she'd looked, he had arms as skinny as pepperami sticks.

"Oh, here you are!"

Owen and Mari turned in unison and were both surprised to see Jack standing there.

"Jack? I thought you were going out with the boys tonight."

"Well, I can catch up with them any night. I quite fancied a session with you two tonight instead!" Jack said kissing Mari on the lips. Mari could see Owen's face darken; it was obvious he didn't want Jack to join them. Perhaps his secret was really sensitive.

"Um, Jack, Owen wanted to discuss something personal with me tonight. If you don't mind giving us a half an hour alone first and then we can join you for a drink later?"

"Oh, OK." Jack was obviously unhappy at this. "I'll go for a pint with Trig then and come back in an hour or so, if that's OK with Owen." Jack gave Owen a baleful look.

"Yeah, fine," Owen said.

"Don't be like that Jack," Mari admonished. "I'll see you later."

Jack nodded curtly and turned on his heel and stalked out of the pub in a snit.

"Sorry about that," Mari said as they sat down with their drinks. "He's not usually like that... So, what's this big thing you wanted to discuss with me? I've been racking my brains all day wondering what you're up to!" She looked at him expectantly.

"Well," Owen paused as he took a big gulp of beer. "Shall we have a cigarette?"

"Why, do I need one?" Mari joked as he lit both cigarettes together and handed her one, his hand shaking slightly.

Owen smiled. 'I've wanted to tell you this for about a year now."

"What? Don't keep me in suspense!" Shit! He didn't have a terminal illness or something did he? Mari's heart started to beat faster as she gazed into his dark brown eyes.

"Well...the thing is...Mari...I love you. I've loved you since the first minute I saw you, although I didn't realise at the time..." He blushed to the roots of his hair and looked intently at his pint as he waited for her to respond.

Mari stared at him in shock. She'd had no idea that he was going to spring this on her. After all, he'd turned her down that one time things could have gone further between them. And now he reckoned he was in love with her!

"You love me?"

"Yes..." Owen said. "I can't help it. I know you and Jack are just 'sex-buddies' and that you're looking for something more serious. Well, I want something more serious too…with you."

Mari was transfixed and decided to let him talk so she could have a bit of time to digest this revelation.

Buoyed by the fact that she hadn't laughed in his face, Owen continued.

"Listen, Mari, I've had my share of women and there was always something wrong with them or with me… I hadn't bothered to get to know them properly first. And once I did get to know them, well I didn't like them… Whilst you and me, well…"

"But you didn't want to go out with me when we went to Boom Box that time…"

"I was scared it would spoil our friendship and we were working together…"

"We still do."

"I don't care any more. I can't bear seeing you with Jack, it's been driving me nuts."

"Is that why you've changed your mind? Because I'm with Jack?"

"It's opened my eyes to how I really feel about you…"

Mari stared at him as if hypnotised. She had thought about Owen as a possible boyfriend, of course, especially when they had that "date" at Boom Box. But after that night, she'd deliberately relegated him to the "friend" category. But what if Owen was the one? Had they really missed their window of opportunity? And what about

Jack? She did like him – lots – didn't she?

"I know what you're thinking," Owen said as if reading her mind. "Have we missed our chance? Do we know each other *too* well? Well, I think being friends first is a really good way to start a lasting relationship."

"But you didn't seem to care when I went out with my ex-es... Before Jack." She'd regularly discussed her relationships with Owen in the past to get the male perspective and he'd never shown an iota of jealousy before, well, until Jack.

"I know, but I didn't know them you see... But Jack's been there in my face every day... And when I saw you both snogging that time... It was horrible."

"Snogging? When?"

"On that bloody steam ship. I wanted to ask you out then, but you were like a heat seeking missile, obsessed with Jack."

Mari's cheeks reddened as she remembered their fight on the boat. She hadn't realised Owen liked her so much.

"I was hoping you felt the same way," Owen said, grabbing her hand. "After all, you hated Lucy."

"Everyone hated Lucy!"

"Mari, we're almost 35. Don't you think it's about time we stopped playing games?"

Before Mari had a chance to respond, she saw Jack walking towards them. His face was white with fury as he clocked that Mari and Owen were holding hands.

"What the fuck's going on here?"

"Jack, what's wrong with you? You're making a scene!"

"I thought there must be something going on between you two." Jack stared at Owen accusingly.

"Listen, Jack. I thought we'd agreed, no strings." Mari said, with the creeping realisation that everyone in the pub was staring at them.

"Yeah, well, I hadn't realised you were such a slag then!"

"Hey, mate," Owen got up. "Watch what you're saying. Don't speak to Mari like that."

"Shut your fuckin' mouth!" Jack yelled at Owen. "I thought you were a good mate, but you're a fuckin' traitor!"

"Stop being so melodramatic, Jack. You've hardly been Mr Innocent since we've been seeing each other. And nothing's been going on between me and Owen anyway!"

"Why were you holding his hand then? And batting your eyelashes at him, eh? You're a slut!" Jack shouted as he closed in on Mari threateningly.

"It's time for you to go," Owen grabbed Jack's arm.

"Don't touch me you twat!"

Before Mari had a chance to say anything, Jack punched Owen squarely in the face and knocked him to the ground.

"Jack!" Mari screamed and pulled him off Owen.

"Hey! Break it up!" A burly bouncer came out of nowhere and grabbed Jack by the scruff of his neck.

"You OK, love?" The bouncer asked Mari, who was on her knees by Owen's side trying to mop up his bloody nose with a hanky.

"Yes. It's him, he's mental!" Mari said, glowering at Jack.

"Mari, please! I'm sorry!" Jack shouted as he was dragged out of the pub. Mari ignored him and turned to Owen.

"Are you OK, Owen?"

"Yeah, I'll be OK in a minute. Little bastard, he caught me unawares…"

It was obvious Owen was embarrassed that Jack had got the better of him.

"Bloody Jack! I never thought he'd be that possessive."

"Well, you were a tad naïve to think you could really have a 'no strings' relationship. Who do you think you are? Samantha in *Sex and the City*?"

"Yeah, right!" Mari said, with a wry smile. "I'm crap with men. Everything always goes tits up!"

"Well, things could be different this time… What do you think?"

"Owen, I don't know. I've had so many bad experiences recently and the last thing I want to do is lose our friendship… It means too much to me."

"Great," said Owen bitterly. "You're quitting before we've started anything. And haven't we done this dialogue before?"

"Yes, we have and I think you were right. It's not my fault that you're almost 35. I don't want to be a consolation prize. I want someone who really wants me, who loves me so much that they can't live without me."

"I do!"

"Yes, of course you do Owen. You want me so much that you turned me down once and you've been seeing other women for as long as we've known each other."

"Well, I didn't realise how I really felt about you… But I *know* now."

"It's not enough, Owen," Mari said, sadly. "I can't afford another catastrophic break up. I've already messed things up with Jack and I'll have to face him at work every day. I can't risk things going awry with us as well. You're too much of a friend for me to risk that. I'm sorry…"

Owen didn't say a word as she reached for her bag and walked out of the pub. She knew she'd made the right decision. She wanted the whole enchilada – the big filmic moment, not an uncertain declaration by a lonely and desperate man. So, why did she feel so bad about it?

Owen

Ms Perfect, 2008

"So, what do we know about Mari?" Huw said matter-of-factly, after listening to Owen's tale of woe.

"That she doesn't want a relationship with me?"

"Not yet. But she will. Leave everything to Uncle Huw. Now, we know that she is a romantic. And that her favourite film of all time is…?"

"*When Harry Met Sally*," Owen finished the sentence sadly.

"And what happens in *When Harry Met Sally*?"

"They're good friends first then after twelve years of faffing about they fall in love. Well, I haven't got twelve years to spare. I'm 34!"

"Yes, yes, I know that. But how does Billy Crystal win Meg Ryan's heart?"

"He runs through the deserted streets on New Year's Eve and tells her how much he loves her?"

"Yes, but not only that. He makes a grand gesture."

"So you're suggesting that I run to Mari's house like a twat and make some idiotic grand gesture?"

"Yes, you have to *show* the girl. You've already *told* her and that didn't work. You need to go bigger!"

"Well, one of the reasons she didn't want to pursue things was that she thought it could cause complications at work…"

"Why don't you quit your job then so you won't have these complications? You hate the job anyway."

"You think that might work?" Owen said hopefully. After all, even if things didn't work with Mari, he didn't want to stay at Celt watching her every day from afar, knowing he couldn't be with her. This might show her he was serious.

"Well, that's a good start, but it's not quite enough. I do have an idea though that might clinch things. Can you borrow an editor on the QT d'you think?"

"Yes, probably but why?"

"You, my little friend, are going to make a movie!"

Finally, D-Day had arrived. Owen had deliberately selected a day when he knew Jack was out on location so he wouldn't spoil the vibe. With the help of Sam, an editor, he'd cut a short film that included all of Mari's favourite clips from some of the most romantic films in history. The scene in *Amélie* where she daydreamed about her perfect day with the man she's loved from afar; where Harry told Sally how he felt about her; the scene in *Dracula* in which Gary Oldman as the young charismatic Impaler told Winona Ryder that he had "crossed oceans of time to be with her," and finally, to seal the deal, where a young, gallant Laurence Olivier as Lord Nelson told Vivien Leigh, his Lady Hamilton, on New Year's Eve 1799 that he'd "kissed her through two centuries." He'd also added a short animated section with a cartoon version of himself revealing his true feelings about her, a lot more eloquently this time. Cheesy, yes, desperate, yes, successful? God, he hoped so.

He was on pins waiting for a chance to get her on her own. At last, he managed to speak to her as they prepared their mid-morning coffees. "Mari, I'm holding a small screening of that short film I've been working on tonight..." He'd already planted the seed that he was preparing a film for a competition. "Can you come and see it? I've asked everyone to stay behind for ten minutes or so after work. It won't take long..." He knew she was free as he'd already checked her online calendar, which was a tad creepy but justifiable in the circumstances.

"Yeah, OK, great," Mari said. "Looking forward, Mr Spielberg!"

He hadn't revealed the contents of the film to anyone apart from Sam, of course, and he'd sworn he wouldn't breathe a word to anyone. The time ticked by unbearably slowly. He kept worrying that Mari wouldn't be able to attend the screening or, horrors, that Jack would return early from his shoot. He tried to get some work done but just couldn't stop thinking about his big plan. Harriet had approached him earlier with a work related query and he'd almost bitten her head off. He'd apologised, but she'd given him some very funny looks afterwards.

Sam had reassured him that everything was fine with

the film and he'd checked the dvd a dozen times in the viewing room. The major worry, of course, was that Mari would laugh in his face along with the rest of the office. Should he go through with it? He decided to ring Huw during his lunch break – he needed reassurance that he was doing the right thing.

"Mate, I don't think I can show it… It's too much of a gamble."

"Don't be a pussy, Owen, you've got to do it. Do you want to lose your woman to this young upstart?"

"What if she thinks it's a joke?"

"She won't you idiot! It's up to you, but if you do pull out, I don't want to hear another word about Mari or about Jack or anything else related to them both! You have a chance here, a chance at everlasting happiness; is extreme cowardice going to stop you?"

"You're right… Thanks mate."

He had to man up. Even if Mari rejected him, at least he'd tried. There was nothing worse than a "What if?" scenario. He didn't want to be watching Mari and Jack getting married from the side lines in a few years' time, past his prime with a paunch, an alcohol problem and a fetching comb-over.

At half past five, Owen got up from his chair and said shouted, "Right, everyone, come and see my film…"

His colleagues slowly made their way to the meeting room where Owen had set up the big screen, some faffing like sheep and chatting instead of making their way quickly.

"Come on, people!" Owen said, trying to hide his impatience. "No, no, not there Harriet!" he said sharply as Harriet tried to park her bottom on the best seat next to the TV. "That's Mari's seat." Harriet tutted but moved to the next seat obediently. Mari sat down in her allotted chair, and gave him a supportive smile. Owen waited for the inevitable coughs, murmurs and chatter to subside and pressed play. He prayed that he wasn't going to make a complete fool of himself in front of everyone but knew it was a risk he had to take. His heart was beating like a drum as the film played. As they reached the end and the animated Owen figure appeared, the room went deathly quiet. Owen looked at his colleagues surreptitiously, he could see that the girls were really taken by the romance of the film and while some of his male colleagues were rolling their eyes, some were quite engrossed. He'd deliberately avoided looking at Mari until the very end. But he then realised everyone else was looking intently, gauging her reaction. He turned slowly to look at her but her face was expressionless apart from a slight redness to her cheeks.

What if she hated it?

And then they came to the best bit, the animated Owen was sharing his true feelings: "Mari, I love you and it's not just because I'm 34 and lonely. It's because of who you are. You can be impatient and naïve at times and a bit pedantic too. But you're also funny, you get my jokes and you have the prettiest eyes I've ever seen. I know you're the girl for me, and I can't just give up and lose you again. Yes, I have been out with a lot of girls and it hasn't worked out because they weren't right for me. And I hope you can see the same thing's happened to you – well you haven't been out with a lot of girls, but you've had a few boyfriends who weren't right for you. It must mean something that we've kept bumping into each other and that our lives have collided so often over the last sixteen or so years... So I made this film *"because when you realise you want to spend the rest of your life with somebody, you want the rest of your life to start as soon as possible."*

Yes, he'd intentionally pinched a line from When Harry Met Sally; he knew Mari always got teary-eyed when Billy Crystal uttered those lines to Meg Ryan at the end of the movie, because she'd told him often enough. Owen looked at Mari again and this time, she was smiling at him. Was this a good sign or was it a "let him down gently" smile? Before she could speak, Owen got up and addressed his audience, "I showed everyone this film because I want to show Mari that I'm deadly serious. I handed in my resignation today in case the fact that we work together complicates things between Mari and me." He turned to Mari and held out his hand nervously. She looked at him and shook her head in disbelief.

Please, please, say yes, please say yes, please…

Mari

Mr Perfect, the same second

Mari looked into Owen's eyes and grabbed the hand he held out before standing up and kissing him like she meant it. For the first time, she knew that this was how true love felt. She'd been carrying around a filmic fantasy of the perfect man with her for twenty years, not realising until now that this mythical faultless creature didn't exist, that he was a fictional creation, not a living, breathing, fallible man of flesh and blood with strengths and weaknesses like everyone else. Yes, Owen could be flaky, a bit immature and sulky at times. But he was also honest, kind, funny and head over heels in love with her. She loved him too, warts and all.

She knew it couldn't have been easy for him to reveal his feelings in front of the whole office. Perhaps he wasn't the perfect man she'd been looking for all these years but she knew he was perfect for her. And she wasn't going to worry about tomorrow, or next year, but live in the moment for once… If things didn't work out, she knew now that she was woman enough to face up to it and go it alone. But as she looked at Owen's grinning face, she had a feeling it would all be, well, perfect.

More from Honno

Short stories; Classics; Autobiography; Fiction

Founded in 1986 to publish the best of women's writing,
Honno publishes a wide range of titles from Welsh women.

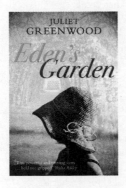

Eden's Garden, *Juliet Greenwood*
Sometimes you have to run away, sometimes you
have to come home: two women a century apart
struggling with love, family duty, long buried
secrets, and their own creative ambitions.
*"Delightful, intriguing tale which unravels family
secrets."* Claire McAlpine, Word by Word
*"A great romantic read and also a very
atmospheric, ingenious mystery."* Margaret James,
Writing Magazine
9781906784355
£8.99

Back Home, by Bethan Darwin
Ellie is brokenhearted and so decamps home.
Tea and sympathy from grandad Trevor help, as
does the distracting and hunky Gabriel, then a
visitor turns Trevor's world upside down...
Winner of the *Pure Gold award*
*"A modern woman's romantic confession,
alongside a cleverly unfolding story of long-buried
family secrets"* Abigail Bosanko
*"Lively, fresh and warm-hearted- an easy-going
and enjoyable read"* Nia Wyn
9781906784034
£8.99

All Honno titles can be ordered online at
www.honno.co.uk
twitter.com/honno
facebook.com/honnopress

Guerrillas in our Midst, by Claire Peate
Edda gets the terrible news that best-friend Beth
is deserting her for family life but a final wine-
fuelled night sees her joining secret group the
Brockley Spades & life gets a lot more exciting…
"*A book to enjoy over a wet weekend with a glass
of bubbly and a big box of chocolates…
Recommended.*" thebookbag.co.uk
"*It's witty and sharp and Peate has an acute eye
for the endless variety of human character*"
Steve Dube, The Western Mail
9781906784256
£8.99

Cold Enough to Freeze Cows, by Lorraine
Jenkin
Iestyn and Menna were schoolfriends, but the
path of true love is a rough farm track. Ladies
man Johnny 'Sandwich' Brechan changes his
ways when his help is called for. Esther is
struggling to love her husband and daughter
and thanks to a computer course has found a
way to vent her spleen at their selfishness and
do some good. Wickedly humorous…
Finalist in *The People's Book Prize*
Highly readable stuff to curl up with…
County Times.
"*Like a Welsh 'Love Actually*"
AB, The Chick Lit Club
(www.chicklitclub.com)
9781906784171
£8.99

All Honno titles can be ordered online at
www.honno.co.uk
twitter.com/honno
facebook.com/honnopress

Chocolate Mousse and Two Spoons, by Lorraine Jenkin
"fun and witty... with many twists in the tale that all women can relate to"
County and Border Life
Lettie Howells has missed her chance – at love, at a career, at life – or so she thinks. A gently humorous take on the perils of dating when you're a flirty over-thirty.
9781870206952
£8.99

More Than Just a Hairdresser, by Nia Pritchard
"Enjoyed it loads. A good juicy read!" Margi Clarke
Mobile hairdresser Shirley and sidekick Oli use the tools of their trade to covertly trail a client's philandering hubbie... A heartwarming belly-laugh of a book.
9781870206853
£6.99

Big Cats and Kitten Heels, by Claire Peate
"Claire Peate writes with wit, affectionate humour and insight"
www.gwales.com
Rachel – suffering from a Dull Life Crisis – embarks on an action-packed hen weekend. But there's a 'big cat' on the loose and only a handsome Welshman in wellies between Rachel and a vicious killer.....
9781870206884
£6.99

The Floristry Commission, by Claire Peate
"...will keep you turning the pages"
South Wales Evening Post
Ros catches her boyfriend making love to her swine of a sister, so runs off to seek solace in the Welsh Marches with old schoolfriend Gloria. But if Ros thought the City was full of intrigue and betrayal, it's got nothing on Kings Newton.
9781870206746
£6.99

All Honno titles can be ordered online at
www.honno.co.uk
twitter.com/honno
facebook.com/honnopress

ABOUT HONNO

Honno Welsh Women's Press was set up in 1986 by a group of women who felt strongly that women in Wales needed wider opportunities to see their writing in print and to become involved in the publishing process. Our aim is to develop the writing talents of women in Wales, give them new and exciting opportunities to see their work published and often to give them their first 'break' as a writer.

Honno is registered as a community co-operative. Any profit that Honno makes is invested in the publishing programme. Women from Wales and around the world have expressed their support for Honno. Each supporter has a vote at the Annual General Meeting.

For more information and to buy our publications, please write to Honno at the address below, or visit our website:

www.honno.co.uk

Honno
Unit 14, Creative Units
Aberystwyth Arts Centre
Aberystwyth
Ceredigion
SY23 3GL

Honno Friends
We are very grateful for the support of the Honno Friends:
Gwyneth Tyson Roberts, Jenny Sabine, Beryl Thomas.

For more information on how you can become a Honno
Friend, see: http://www.honno.co.uk/friends.php